I0626535

Responses from Excited Readers

You are instantly connected to the stories and the storyteller, in this quick read, through the imagery and analogies. You are immediately drawn in and though you may not want to, you are forced to join the Fringe - a secret society. In this read, I journeyed with the members and I was enlightened. My veil of ignorance was removed. I understood.

You rally, you cheer, and you hope for those who desire to be free of the Fringe. You feel compassion for those who do not have the will to escape it and you are angered by the roadblocks from society, obstructing their deliverance. How will you feel when you choose to walk a mile with them? How will you decide? What will your actions be?

Preconceived notions of what it means to live on the streets takes on a completely new reality. It makes the possibility of you personally becoming homeless, a believable outcome. This is a read for anyone who thinks they already know the definition of who a homeless person is. You say, " I could never be homeless?" Think again ...

Kimberly Flagler Heiple, degree in English Lit, mother of 2

Renee Crosby takes you from one person's story to the next. Through these stories, she tries to explain to the reader that homelessness, like many social issues, cannot be attributed solely to one cause. While addressing one symptom may help an individual, it is impossible to eradicate homelessness until there is enough research to fully understand it from a big picture perspective. One thing that comes through loud and clear is that until we get back to extended families helping families, there will continue to be a need for shelters, food banks and government assistance. The topic of homelessness is often controversial and keeping an open mind is important to the analysis and eventual resolution of the issue. Not everyone will agree with Renee's stance on how society can help, but it is the start of a discussion that must continue if we are ever to defeat this problem. We as a society must figure out the best way to eradicate homelessness, giving back in many cases not just at Christmas but year round.

Julie Isom, mother of two, Satellite Beach, FL

This is a non-stop book. I picked it up and read it through in one seating. I couldn't put it down as tears filled my eyes and I felt a new kinship with the secret society at the fringe of my world. I read this one Sunday morning before church and was inspired to challenge our congregation to be more attentive to persons on the fringe. My heart was touched. This book awakens sensitivity, convicts the conscience, and softens the heart. It invites us to contemplate the realities of the fringe and then move to action to respond with love, generosity, and social concern.

This text may open you to a world you've tried to avoid or overlooked on your way to work or at the coffee shop. It will open your heart to Jesus' affirmation that *as you have done unto to the least of these, my brothers and sisters, you have done unto me.* You will be richer by encountering the people of the fringe.

Dr Bruce Epperly, pastor, teacher, and author of over 25 books, including *Process Theology: Embracing Adventure with God* and *Finding God in Suffering: A Journey with Job*

The Fringe recounts the stories of the homeless through the eyes of someone on the "inside." An opera singer who found herself on hard times, attempts to bring to the reader the experiences of other seemingly "normal" people, who for various reasons find themselves homeless as well.

The author helps to put a face of humanity on this population in our society, who many times go unnoticed or ignored. Through honest stories with stark realities, she also helps us to understand that we are not so different from these people, and that perhaps we are all just one bad break away from finding ourselves as members of the fringe.

The reader is challenged to see things differently, feel things differently and to ultimately react differently. If you have not had the opportunity to connect with the members of "the fringe," this book will help to break down barriers and preconceived notions, such that you just might leave the fear and judgment behind, and find the courage to reach out and become a friend of the fringe (FOF).

Carol Alexander, Family Promise Volunteer, Denver, CO

As I read *The Fringe*, I found myself entering another world. A world that co-exists with the "regular" world but is seldom truly seen and rarely understood. This book shows the bittersweet lives that are lived out of desperation and necessity in which a soul has forgotten how to dream, how to live in the open, and how to do anything but survive. Renee has captured the quiet courage and made that world become visible to those who would live with the blinders of judgment and prejudice. May God bless her in her work.

Rev. Shauna Hyde
Pastor First United Methodist Church, Ravenswood, WV &
author of *Fifty Shades of Grace* and *Vicar of Tent Town*

Author, Renee Crosby, captures the courage of one woman's brave spirit to reveal the truth about a secret society that surrounds all of our lives. Undoubtedly, through the authors own experiences or incredible imagination, we come to understand that the society is secret because we choose it to be. Homelessness, and all that associated with it— like hunger, shame, judgment, stigma, and a continued cycle of despair, to name a few— is difficult to witness.

As our character's life as an accomplished opera singer declines and twists into a seemingly unavoidable and inescapable demise, she becomes simultaneously disgusted and emboldened by her experiences and observations and shares the stories of The Fringe.

These tales break the silence, attempting to destroy the society's secrecy and let the world know who they really are. It's time to bridge the gap between awareness, understanding, and humanity. It's time for the world to know about the Fringe.

Deren Abram, *Film Pharm*

The Fringe shines a spotlight on those living in the shadows of society. The stereotypes of all displaced or homeless people choosing to be on the streets or living in shelters trying to get their next drink or fix are quickly dispelled. Some members of the fringe are drug addicts or alcoholics. Many others, however, fled physical or sexual abuse, lost a job, were evicted from a home, faced overwhelming financial hardships, or suffer from physical or mental conditions without meaningful treatment options. People living in the fringe include children, military vets, single mothers and the elderly. They once lived like other people with a place to call home, schools for their children and little worry about their future.

Through the personal and true accounts of people who found themselves homeless, The Fringe describes the struggles of those trying to emerge out of their situation. The reader learns of the shame, the constant fear for one's safety, and of the anger and guilt of living on the outside looking in. Many people living a "normal" life are only a few paychecks, an abusive event or a medical condition away from being homeless. Once living in the shadows, the challenges faced in finding work and a place to call their own are often overwhelming.

After reading *The Fringe*, one will look at those all around us living on the streets or in shelters in a whole new light. In a nation so blessed, the fact that America has so many homeless is a sad commentary on our values. The Fringe is a call to action. With understanding and compassion, we can lift those living in the shadows out of their despair and homelessness and bring them back into the mainstream of society.

Brian K. Hugen, Esq,
Hugen Law Firm, LLC, Denver, CO

The Fringe was a very educational, eye opener, quick read... Renee did a spectacular job at taking us on a journey and letting us spend time in the characters' shoes from the comfort of our homes, and coffee shops. The characters seem to reach from the pages and say we are here and hopefully you will all have a better understanding of what it's really like for people who live in the fringe....the synopses of these people from all walks of life are short, well written and easy to follow... It is like being there long enough to say wow I get how things can get so complicated... Like the girl whose purse was stolen while sleeping under the bridge... No ID, no way to move forward...no way to prove who she is...it is hard to let go of the characters at the end of the chapters because you want so badly for good things to come to them. Renee did a good job at that transition though with famous quotes and statements. It is a reality based book which really transcends the message of hope and understanding to all who read it. Thank you Renee, for sharing your knowledge and compassion for the people in the fringe.

Marla Habitz

Renee Crosby's book, *The Fringe*, reaffirms the belief that each person is born with dignity and deserves to be treated with dignity no matter what their circumstances. This book reveals the road-blocks and difficulties people on the fringe of our society are faced with everyday. It challenges readers to overcome preconceived ideas about homelessness without judgment through education on those issues. If you have ever wondered why that person on the street corner isn't working at a "real job," this book will expose you to possible reasons why or how they came to be on that street corner.

Mary Frances Tharp
Executive Director, Boys Hope Girls Hope

The Fringe, written from a unique perspective, will change the way that you look and feel about the homeless epidemic in our country. The fringe examines the struggles that the homeless endure and shows what a difference a small amount of compassion can make in their lives.

Janet Randles, resort sales representative

Famous Former Fringe Members

(Look for more information at the end of the book.)

Steve Jobs
Steve Harvey
Jim Carrey
Kelly Clarkson
Michael Oher (*The Blind Side* movie)
Halle Berry
Jewel
Chris Gardner (*The Pursuit of Happiness* movie)
Ella Fitzgerald
Cappadonna
Kurt Cobain
Harry Houdini
Kelsey Grammer
2Pac
David Letterman
Lil'Kim
William Shatner
Al Pacino
Hillary Swank
Shania Twain
Jennifer Lopez
Drew Carey
Margot Kidder
Sugar Ray Williams
Willie Aames
Suze Orman
Daniel Craig
Phil McGraw (*Dr. Phil*)

RENEE CROSBY

... is a breast cancer survivor, author with three published works, former career woman, married in mid 30's, gone mad as a housewife (just ask my husband of over 12 years), mother of 2, often 3, and sometimes 4, interior decorator, and self-proclaimed advocate for the homeless.

THE FRINGE

A Secret Society

My Eyes, Their Stories

Renee Crosby

Energion Publications
Gonzalez, FL
2015

Copyright © 2015, Renee Crosby

Cover Design: Renee Crosby & Henry Neufeld

ISBN10: 978-1-63199-127-2
ISBN13: 1-63199-127-1
Library of Congress Control Number: 2015933088

Energion Publications
P. O. Box 841
Gonzalez, FL 32560
850-525-

energionpubs.com
pubs@energion.com

Dedicated to social justice seekers everywhere.

"I raise my voice not so that I can shout,
but so that those without a voice can be heard"
— Malala Yousafzai

Table of Contents

1 ✶ The Secret Society

labaster skin is what I have. If you have ever seen an opera singer, you might expect my skin to look like that. It was like I was destined from birth to be an opera singer. And a trained opera singer I became, a soprano no less. It's important for you to know a few other things about me. I am in my early twenties. I am a single mom of a delightful two year old son. I am very smart, attractive, nice, personable, resourceful, educated and strong. You can almost hear the song playing in the background … *I'm every woman...* by Whitney Houston. It may seem as if I am like every woman, but I am not. I have a dark side that most don't have and couldn't even imagine.

I am a member of The Fringe, a secret society. As I write my story and the stories of other members of our secret society, know that you will never know who I am. I cannot share my identity or even my first name. I cannot even risk giving myself a pseudo first name. If I did, I would suffer great persecution and judgment.

American Express claims, "Membership has its privileges," well for us that is not true. Our membership comes with isolation, darkness, silence, judgment and shame. I am tired of carrying the burden of our invisible existence among you. I will not hide our secrets any longer. It is time you knew our stories and the truth of who we really are.

What we aren't. The Fringe isn't one of those fancy social clubs like the Red Hat Ladies. Our Society isn't much like the Rotary Club either. Nor are we like exclusive private clubs with a fifteen year waiting list, fine leather chairs and gleaming mahogany surrounding us. We are not a politically founded group, although there are certainly the politics of The Fringe Society. We don't require membership dues, although we do pay a high price for our standard of living. We are not organized based on charitable acts for the philanthropic endowment of children's hospitals like the Scottish Rite.

As with many secret societies a symbol is often used to identify the group. Those symbols may be known to the masses in general, or may be known only to the members. For instance, a swastika is known the world over for its association with the Nazis. OK, so one could argue the society wasn't so secret, but their heinous activities were. Unlike the familiarity of the swastika, the symbols for American gangs like the Bloods or the CRIPS are extremely hard to identify, even for law enforcement that may be trained to recognize them.

That being said, as with other secret societies we too have an associated symbol with our secret society, The Fringe. Most reading this will not have heard of our plight or know our society's symbol. As part of my pilgrimage to bring us out of the darkness, I will share with you that our symbol is the crescent moon. If you would look at the beginning of each chapter, you will see it.

As with any chosen symbol, ours has great meaning in selection. It really is a perfect representation of those of us living in The Fringe. That crescent moon mysteriously hangs in the sky ostensibly. At first glance it seems to be "on its own" but after further scrutiny, you can see that it's a small part attached to the whole moon.

We are The Fringe, called this because we live on the edge of a so called normal life and on the edge of accepted cultural standards.

Some of us function in circles of normal and you don't even know that we are members of The Fringe. It's natural for us to put on a front when one has to deal with the consequences of a cultural standard of normal, especially when you're not *normal*.

I mean, what the hell is normal anyway? What a great ambiguous term! It's like when you were in high school – normal was set by "the group." They were the measuring stick by which all others were measured.

You remember in high school, you tried to dress like them. You tried to have the same friends as them. You wanted to hang out where they did. You may have wanted to play the sports they played. You wished you could sit at "their" table at lunch. You wanted to be in the clubs they were in... remember that feeling of trying to fit into normal?

I even remember being in high school in the Midwest and joining the ski club. I had never been skiing. I had not planned to go skiing. I couldn't afford to ski even if I wanted to. But, all the cool kids were in ski club. So I joined. Well, we never move too far from this in our society. Normal is set by the group. The rest of us just try to fit in.

My point is this, for those of us in The Fringe Society we are on the outside looking in. Imagine a beautiful building labeled "normal" where most of society lives. I am the one who will go into the building via the *normal* push/pull door to get you. I will bring you outside the building via that push/pull door for you to watch what it is like to try to jump back through the *other* door.

The other door is designed for those traveling with a heavy load that has their hands full. It's the circular revolving door. You know the one where kids like to play. The one that if it's moving too fast from a running, rotating child, you can't enter until it slows.

Somehow in the way of revolving doors, we got shoved outside of the building. There is born The Fringe, a secret society. With our hands full from a heavy load, we are just trying to jump back through a fast moving circular, revolving door. We would do anything to time it just right, to jump into the revolving door and get back inside.

Why are we on the outside or how did we get here? Good questions. You should be asking questions. That is the point of sharing my story. We are in The Fringe because at some point in time, our lives took a turn for the worst. Many of us have teetered

3

on the edge of normal for a while. Then we succumbed to the undertow of what ails us, finding ourselves trapped in the rip tide of life. Once in the sea of The Fringe, we live a shameful existence much like the slaves of the Underground Railroad.

Like them, our lives are carried out in secret and we most prevalently live in disguise, cloaked among you. We are despised for our membership and our plight is often misunderstood like them. And like the slaves navigating the Underground Railroad, we too live in constant fear.

Luckily, like those of the Underground Railroad, we too have friends of The Fringe that help us to obtain freedom from what oppresses us. Many of our stories show the kindness of these friends and strangers helping us. Perhaps once you read this, you will join us in our fight to become free from judgment and embrace understanding and compassion.

You must be informed of the unjust nature of our condemnation. We should not hang our heads low for the fear or the shame of being found out. Perhaps it is normal society that should fear the shame of being found out for its abhorrent, intolerant, ignorant behavior. Regular society doesn't welcome, want or know what to do with us.

Do not be baffled that we are among you and that you don't even know of our secret society. That is understandable since we are really not much different than you. We too used to live in the same beautiful building labeled *normal*. We are opera singers (myself), retired military, painters, stay at home moms, high level police officers, senior care takers, construction workers, machinist, immigrant grandmothers, chefs and even teachers.

We, The Fringe, are among you, in the midst of your daily life. We are the ones sitting near you on a chair at Starbucks. We are the ones in line next to you at the grocery store. We are the women sitting next to you at the park watching our children play. We are the people at the gym working out near you. We are the people who served the country in the military, and teach your children at school.

It is these men and women's stories of whom I will tell. Remember, I am an opera singer, not a writer. With that in mind, I share this compilation of their short stories through my eyes. I will give each person a pseudo name for their story. But know that any similarity with someone you may have personally met, or might meet, in the Secret Society of The Fringe, is just a coincidence.

It is with that hope that I have chosen to intersect our lives. It occurred to me that an enlightened perspective is all that you need. It's not your fault that we live in shame. It's not your fault that you don't know who we are. I mean, you can't fix something unless you know it's broken. That's why I have chosen to enlighten normal society of our presence in the world.

I write because I refuse to hide our secrets any more. I will not be silent any longer. I am tired of living in secrecy and shame. I am tired of coveting the temporary failure of our lives and our cloaked existence among you. It is time for society to learn what is wrong with ignorance so that it can be fixed.

All I'm asking is that you come to pay attention to those outside the building with heavy loads that are trying to jump through that fast revolving door. I hope that perhaps one day you will walk over to slow the revolving door so that we can safely get back in.

In the end, I hope there is compassion and awareness for those of us in The Fringe. Perhaps one day there will be no need for our secret society. I can only hope.

We dance round in a ring and suppose,
but the secret sits in the middle and knows.

— Robert Frost[1]

---

1   http://www.brainyquote.com/quotes/quotes/r/robertfros151827.html

2 I JOIN THE FRINGE

Although I knew I was destined to be an alabaster-skinned, soprano opera singer, I had never envisioned being destined to join The Fringe. I was like you. I didn't even know that the secret members of The Fringe Society were all around us.

I grew up in a rather normal middle class family. I went to college. I have a bachelor's degree. I did all the usual things women do. After having graduated from college I sang my heart out. Being a soprano these days has advantages and disadvantages. One of the perks is hanging out with more mature people. At least I think that is a perk. Most young women in their twenties wouldn't think hanging out with older people would be desirable let alone enjoyable. But you have to admit, to have the desire and courage to become an opera singer is not typical for a twenty year old either. I am rather mature for my age.

It shouldn't surprise you much to know that my singing career landed me in New England. This was the hub for opera singers to live and work. It shouldn't surprise you either that I soon married a man almost twice my age. Early in our marriage we had a child as well. That is when I stopped working outside of the home.

That is when I became the persona of Julia Roberts when she played the wife, Laura Burney, in the movie *Sleeping with the Enemy*. If you have never seen the movie, it is about an older man married to a young woman. The marriage is about control. Somewhere it subtly and quickly turns ugly. It turns abusive. It turns violent.

Like Julia Roberts character, Laura, living with abuse, I seemed to have only one option. I had to escape. I had to run. I had to disappear with my son.

I prepared, like Laura. Then, like Laura, one day we did it. I took my son and we escaped. I went from a respectable stay at home mom and opera singer to a member of the secret society The Fringe at age 23.

I prepared, but couldn't have prepared for life in the Fringe. I had no idea what obstacles I would face. In seconds my lifestyle took a drastic change to living in a way that I knew not how to live. But, I knew in my heart it was better than the abuse from where I came. I was officially... (hesitation, rapid heartbeat, fear, breathe, focus, be daring, spread hope)... homeless.

Should I let you digest that a minute? Yes, all the members of The Fringe are homeless. That is the connecting link in our secret society. That is the shame that not only bonds us but labels us. That is the shame in which we are judged by. The stereotypes culture has placed on the homeless are what we are scrutinized, condemned and painfully branded with. I know you already have a preconceived notion of our "kind." That is the point of me breaking the silence to increase the awareness and knowledge of who we really are. It is time for the truth.

Am I not what you expected as far as homeless people go? I thought not. Neither will any of the other people's stories that I will share. In my case, I am not alone in how I became a member of The Fringe. The eye awakening fact is that nineteen percent of single homeless people are victims of domestic violence.[2] So, I come to share my story with you so that you will learn of our plight, our real plight, not the assumed stereotypical societal image of us, the homeless.

Let me get back to my joining The Fringe. The first thing I did with a large portion of my cash money was to buy another car so

---

2   http://www.nationalhomeless.org/factsheets/who.html

that my abusive husband wouldn't know what we were driving. I knew he would have the police looking for us. Not only did I need a new car for disguise, I needed a new car that was dependable. I needed to get as far away from New England as I could.

Journey we did. We crossed many bridges, highways and state lines. We had ended up in a major western city, living in a hotel room. Yes, me and a **very** active two year old. Yes, please imagine that. All we have is strapped to our backs or the car. There is a limited amount of books, toys and things you can bring on the run to keep a two year old busy in a one room hotel.

Now, imagine some of my challenges. I need to find a job. I have many talents, a college degree and a good solid work record. Ever tried to look for a job with a two year old with you 24/7? I pursue employment, walking to many businesses, with said two year old in tow. Just trying to speak with a secretary and obtaining an application and filling it out in an office while trying to entertain and keep quiet a two year old is **difficult**. Frustrating doesn't begin to describe my emotions.

The result of most of those on site applications is, "No interview today. We'll call you." Panic sets in, call me? How long before they figure out by dialing my number that I am a guest at a hotel? Oh that will help my chances of getting an interview. I had already worried whether they would know the address on the application as a hotel. If they put two and two together, they will certainly figure out that I am currently homeless. If they figure out I am currently homeless, I don't have a chance.

So, trying to exude confidence and an expectant demeanor of "getting a phone call,"—I exit. I can barely breathe. Note to self, get cell phone for next time. At least I am one of the lucky ones that can afford a cell phone for the time being. Maybe with my own number but still a hotel address, maybe then they won't figure out I am homeless. I wonder if 10 digits can make the perceived difference between homeless and not?

After several applications, would you believe I got an interview? OK, so taking my rambunctious two year old while filling out applications was painful but doable; I cannot take my son on an interview. Now I need to figure out what to do with my son when I go. I am in a new city with no one to lend a hand. I am alone. I can't leave him in the hotel room by himself. I can't leave him in the car either. And I certainly can't leave him with my "neighbor" at the hotel.

Enter friends of The Fringe. I have a friend in another state who knows someone who lives in the city where I am presently staying. We make a connection. She agrees to help and watch my son while I interview and look for a job. Yes, I am really leaving my child with a complete stranger. Please don't judge me. My friend is her friend, and I really trust her opinion. A girl's gotta do what a girl's gotta do. The desperation and overwhelming circumstances of looking for a job as a lone sole parent are temporarily relieved. I have someone to lean on, to help.

No, I didn't get the job. The disappointment is behind me, and I will continue to search. As expected with the fringing life, there are other challenges to address. I have two other problems to deal with. I have expired temporary tags and I have been evicted from my hotel room, the shame of it all.

You have no idea. That is why I am sharing my story, so that you will come to understand our lives. I have paid my hotel bill on time and in full. I am not being evicted as you would assume for nonpayment. The reason I am being evicted from my hotel room is that there is a big event in town for the coming weekend. I can either accept their raise in rate over the weekend, double what I normally pay, or I can leave.

Funds are limited. I can't be stupid. I must accept the inconvenience and pack up our stuff. So, I have to spend four hours packing our belongings and shoving them into every crevice of the car to move on for the next few nights. Oh, and try entertaining a 2 1/2 year old while packing and shoving a room full of things into a Subaru Outback. So, the car is loaded and we make our way further out of town so as to not be gouged with high hotel bills for the event weekend. The bright side is that maybe if I am lucky, the rural police will have less of a chance of pulling me over for expired tags.

Speaking of my expired temporary plates, I have some money set aside to get the new plates. Even though I had thoroughly planned for our life on the run, unexpected challenges arrive from a fringing lifestyle. Being part of this secret society, I don't think I could have anticipated some of the hurdles I face on a daily basis.

Today is one of those days. After having been to the Department of Motor Vehicles where I waited two and a half hours with my sometimes not so delightful nap deprived two year old, I was informed I can't get new plates. I hope you are asking yourself, why not?

Good question. It's not a matter of money for me, although that can be an issue for many in my position. You see, I have to have a valid in-state driver's license to get a license plate. Then go get the new state's driver's license, right? To have a valid driver's license, I have to have proof of residence. Well that seems simple enough. But I can't prove my residence because of some erroneous antiquated state standard. Unfortunately, a hotel address is not proof of residency. I don't have a lease or a utility bill to prove my residence. I cannot obtain a valid driver's license for the new state I am living in. Therefore, I cannot obtain license plates. It's that simple.

This might not seem like a big deal to you. But, the one last thing I own, that I can call my own, that validates me as a functioning member of society, my car, now has me on the wrong side of the law. It complicates the simplest of things in a long list of complicated things for a homeless woman and her son. It's humiliating. It's devaluing. It's embarrassing. Not only am I homeless, but a small time criminal as well—a step towards the deadbeat homeless person we are stereotyped as.

I believe I have spent enough time on the key components of my story that you needed to hear about. I don't like being the focus of such scrutiny anyway. So, let's move on. There are so many other challenges for those of us in The Fringe Society to share with you. I hope to do justice to the stories of these others. May my sharing of their stories in some small way validate who they are as valued, loving, and impactful people? All of them I encountered in The Fringe changed my life. Just maybe they will change yours. So, please grab a cup of coffee and read on, by all means.

> *"There is no value in life*
> *except what you choose to place upon it*
> *and no happiness in any place*
> *except what you bring to it yourself."*
> – Henry David Thoreau[3]

---

3   http://www.brainyquote.com/quotes/keywords/value.html

3 ★ ONE BAD APPLE

You may have never had earwigs come spilling out of a peach, but everyone has probably cut or bitten into an apple to find a worm. So, do you believe that one bad apple (or peach) spoils the whole bunch?

I was cutting open a peach for morning breakfast. My son was watching intently with his eyes dancing with happiness, taste buds anticipating and drool forming in his mouth like Pavlov's dogs waiting for the delectable peach. Down goes the knife. Just like a horror film of our own, the peach came alive, spilling with frantically crawling earwig bugs all over the cutting board and counter. We both scream and jump around like Mexican jumping beans until I kill all of the bugs.

Needless to say, I was possessed to throw away the whole box of perfectly ripe peaches. I didn't have the restraint to rationalize that the others were perfectly fine and cost good money. As well, my son hasn't wanted peaches since then. This is not a real surprise.

Visions dance in our head of all those slimy creepy things crawling out of our food. When I buy peaches now, I am the only one eating them for breakfast, lunch and snack to get rid of them before they spoil. But, as you might expect, each time I cut one open, I cringe. Who knows when my son will eat a peach again? It may just be one of those moments he won't forget, and when he is an adult and has kids and is cutting a peach, he will tell the story again. His kids will be like, "We know, Dad, and we've heard this story forty times before!"

If you are like me, you would rather pass on the rest of those associated with the original bad peach, or apple! It's in our nature. The experience left me with a lifelong peach cut-cringe. Or, if you are like my son, a lifelong aversion to all of them has been established. He may never eat a peach again. Natural aversion to the whole kind may happen. This is a worthy point to contemplate regarding those of us fringing.

I believe that one bad apple doesn't spoil the whole bunch but it sure makes it hard to get past the aversion to enjoy the other ones. Let's face it, there are stereotypes of the homeless, and often those stereotypes impact one's perception of *all* homeless people. But it's important to become aware of one's natural aversion and to learn to identify with that uncomfortable feeling; to reach in the basket with one bad apple, and to be able to pull out many other glorious, ripe, juicy apples one would otherwise miss.

Stereo types abound that we aren't even aware which culture subtly places in our minds. For example, I was watching a movie with my young son. This movie was produced by Disney. Needless to say, I was sorely disappointed that during the movie they had two references to those in economic despair, or the less fortunate. They used the words "hobo" and "homeless lady wrapped in a blanket." BAM! Right there. Did you have a visual of a "hobo" or a "homeless lady wrapped in a blanket.?" What did they look like? What was on their feet? What did their faces look like? What kind of clothing did they have on? What was their hair like? What was their facial expression? I admit that I too have a visual. It's called a stereotype. No worries, we all have them. We can't help but have them with our cultural, media and socially developed views.

If you grew up in the seventies, hobo was a common phrase for the homeless. There were so few. Or, so it seemed. You never actually saw a hobo. But if you did, you would have known it immediately by their appearance. It wasn't even politically incorrect to talk about them or to dress up like one for Halloween.

As a group they were few and far between. You didn't see them on the street corners. You didn't see them in the downtown cities. Back in the day, if I wanted to see or meet one, I would have gone to a nearby railroad or a park bench where I would expect to find a "bum." How about you? Where would you have looked for one? That's a far cry from where we find homeless people today. They are on almost all street corners. Ever wonder why or what changed?

As the years go by, the social terms evolve with the stereotypes. In the past the colloquial term may have been "bum," but not now. Too often I have seen articles in the paper or on the Internet about *vagrants*. No human being should be referred to as a vagrant. The term is deplorable, dignity-defying and downright mean.

If you search for that word on the Internet, most articles about *vagrants* are about the homeless. OK – almost *all* of them are about the homeless. I just hate to use an all-inclusive word like *all*. But it's true.

So, what's my point? The point is that we *all* (there I said it again) have a stereotype in our mind of the homeless. Our stereotypes can be based on what we think they look like, or how they got to be homeless, or why they must be homeless. BAM! Right there. It happened again. Did you just think about a typical lazy, opportunist who mooches off of society and our welfare system? How about visualizing a typical panhandling addict who is begging for money on the side of the road to only be used for his next fix? It's not a hard stretch is it?

The point of addressing one's culturally ingrained stereotypes is crucial in the battle of mitigating the harsh judgment on members of The Fringe. Yes. I don't deny that there are those that do fit a stereotype, but that is only a small portion of the homeless in our country.

My story and these other stories through my eyes are shared to dispel the myths and stereotypes of who and why the homeless are the homeless. May our truth become known? May you be one step closer to not being so quick to judge when you hear the word "homeless." Dare I wish out loud that you will become more compassionate for those living in The Fringe.

> *"Three things cannot be long hidden:*
> *the sun, the moon, and the truth".*
> — Buddha[4]

4   http://www.brainyquote.com/quotes/keywords/moon.html

4 Love in the Fringe

riends of The Fringe (FOF) encountered this lovely couple. The FOF were doing a book club with some women in an emergency shelter. Yes, we even read books and have book clubs just like everyone else. At the end of club time one of the women says, "I am working on something exciting today. I am trying to get enough extra money to pay for a marriage license to marry the father of my two children, the love of my life. We have finally decided to tie the knot!"

That was exciting news. Who doesn't enjoy a good sappy love story? But the friends of The Fringe thought it was rather odd of the couple's single-mindedness to have a wedding right now. Shouldn't they be focused on getting out of their homeless situation?

FOF knew hard times had fallen on the couple. They had lost their home due to employment difficulties. Not only was it bad enough that they had no place to sleep, but the fact that there is no shelter for this family to stay together is heartbreaking. This particular shelter is for women and children only. The bride was staying at the shelter with the two young children, and the father was sleeping in the car in the parking lot at night.

As FOF thought, you too might think they would be focused on finding shelter for the family, as a unit, instead of being separated every night. One would think they would be focused on lifting themselves out of this desperate homeless situation by looking for a job.

It just goes to show that unless we walk a mile in their shoes, we really can't relate. The fact that this woman was only focused on wanting to honor her family and the father of her children by marrying the man she loved, was the lesson to be learned by the FOF.

This lesson is about how becoming a member of the secret society of The Fringe had changed this couple's vision. It cemented their actions to match their values. All that mattered at the moment was being bonded together in holy matrimony.

The bride said, "We know we are only temporarily homeless. We will get out of The Fringe, but when we do, we want to be one. Now more than ever we realize how lucky we are to have each other and these two beautiful children. Really, if we have each other, we have what matters most—love." Sounds like a perfect episode to run on the 70's show *The Love Boat*, am I right?

How could the FOF not be inspired and humbled by this quirky single-minded focus on marriage? So, get this, it was 4PM in the afternoon when this love story whacked the FOF on the head. They got it... a wedding needed to happen. The frenzy started. Come hell or high water the friends of The Fringe were banding together to set in motion this couples' unity in marriage.

So, FOF gathered them and asked if they could give them a wedding. The couple was in tears, and said yes. Saying yes was not as easy as one would think for a newly homeless couple. They had not experienced the gracious generosity of complete strangers before, nor had they expected such kindness. It was humbling but validating somehow. So, the wedding was set for the next morning at 10:00 a.m.

As the FOF worked on putting the wedding together, they found out that the groom had been seeking God. In his quest, he was led to a pastor of a small local church near the shelter. FOF found out from the pastor that money had already been secured to get the marriage certificate.

The beauty of this is that the father had already begun to work on putting into motion a wedding for the couple. He wanted to surprise his bride. He was planning a small ceremony to get married much to the bride's unknowing. The father of the children wanted to honor the mother of his children with what she wanted most, to be joined in marriage without wasting another minute being separate.

Perhaps it was being physically separated with one in a shelter and one in a car that moved them to do whatever they could to be joined as one in marriage. Their reality had changed. There was a paradigm shift. Their morals and life principles as *normal* members of society were being challenged. Their lives were actually enriched by being homeless.

So, off and running the FOF went. By nine o'clock that night all items had been *given* to make the bride's wedding a dream. A local bridal shop is first on the list. No woman can have a wedding without *the* dress. She is whisked away to a fitting room after having selected a few bridal gowns to try on. The owner of the shop says he would gladly give the bride whatever dress she wanted. As tears ran down her face, she said, "Really, may I have this one?" To which he replies, "Yes." It was a beautiful ivory wedding gown with a flowing train.

A few wet tissues later, FOF is back on the mission. Next, they secured flowers, also donated by a local shop. After a few phone calls and a quick trip to the mall, money is donated and the children have fancy new clothes for the ceremony. Enough money is given by complete strangers that FOF also had the couple pick out wedding bands. After dropping off the overwhelmed couple, FOF finishes preparing for the wedding by getting food, the wedding cake, candles, and some decorations for the church!

The next morning, all goes as planned. The bride dresses and puts on makeup. Pictures are taken with her and the children. The music starts. The children adorn the aisle with flower petals. The bride cascades down the aisle to meet her groom. The couple is married amidst a few new friends and with family on their cell phone. It was truly one of the most beautiful ceremonies I had ever witnessed.

After that day the FOF wedding brigade never saw the couple again as it often goes in these cases of kindness to members of the homeless community. But, word eventually traveled back to the wedding FOF. The couple and their children are happy. The husband finally found another job. They were lifted out of their desperate situation, and now owned their own home and live happily ever after.

Having shared their love story, you have gotten a glimpse of a different version of the homeless that you may have not known before, the temporarily displaced average American family. Surprisingly, they are a common occurrence in our secret society.

The number of homeless families with children has increased significantly over the past decade. Families with children are among the fastest growing segments of the homeless population. In its 2007 survey of 23 American cities, the U.S. Conference of Mayors found that families with children comprised 23% of the homeless population (U.S. Conference of Mayors, 2007). These proportions are likely to be higher in rural areas. Research indicates that families, single mothers, and children make up the largest group of people who are homeless in rural areas (Vissing, 1996).[5]

The tragic part of this, while these statistics show that families are an increasing part of the homeless population, the figures do not yet take into account the catastrophic effect of the mortgage crisis on the secret society. When those figures are available, I think all will be shocked at the impact on the average American family.

"I met in the street a very poor young man who was in love.
His hat was old, his coat worn, his cloak was out at the elbows,
the water passed through his shoes,
—and the stars through his soul."
— Victor Hugo[6]

---

5   http://www.nationalhomeless.org/factsheets/who.html
6   http://www.brainyquote.com/quotes/keywords/shoes.html

5 The Gifted Woman

Have you ever met someone that was so talented at something that it blew your mind away? I have run into many talented people. There are many different kinds of talents. There are people that are book smart and some that are street smart. Those that are book smart, as well as street smart, just seem to "get it." They excel in knowledge, like Albert Einstein. Know what I mean?

Beyond those knowledge gurus, there are other kinds of talented people. There are natural born sellers, and gifted, amazing athletes. Then there are people with astonishing musical talent. I am sure we can all agree on gifted musicians such as Bach and Mozart, or is it Tim McGraw and Adele?

What I see as the key to all of these highly talented people is a natural talent, or a special mojo, if you will. These talented people would have the talent whether they pursued to cultivate and develop their finite skills or not.

The other common component of these talented people is pure passion. Let me be clear. I am not talking about the kind of determination that pushes someone to spend 500 waking hours a month practicing a sport to excel at a position. I am not talking about someone who desires to be an astronaut that cultivates this dream through years of education, reading, networking and training. I am not talking about someone who would do anything to win a game, including bribing a coach to throw a game. That kind of talent, fueled by determination, is different than pure passion. It is limited in that it's a means to an end. Inherently the goal of the development of the talent slants towards a selfish goal—to excel, win or be the best at all costs. Not that there is anything wrong with that.

If we could just agree that there is just a marked difference between altruistic born talents driven by passion versus talent driven by determination to excel.

The kind of passion the aforementioned gifted persons have, like Einstein and Mozart, is a different kind of passion. Theirs is a passion fueled by an inherent, altruistic trigger. That trigger is just the passion of their minds natural focus. They seek to fulfill their destiny and utilize their gifts and talents for the benefit and the good of the world around them.

For Einstein, his trigger was not to obtain a Nobel peace prize and accolades for being a genius. I mean talk about a guy with mojo. He not only was a genius in physics, but was socially gifted in understanding people, their culture and what makes them tick. He was a balanced man of intense book smarts and "people smarts"—a true rare combination. If you ever have a chance to read some of his writings on his philosophies on people, faith and culture, pick up *Ideas and Opinions* that contains some of his personal essays.

My fascination for Einstein aside, this is the kind of natural gift alluded to when I tell you about my friend Sabrina. She is a young woman I met at a women's shelter. She is a total joy, age 24, tall and slender, a gentle giant of a stunning woman, with a heart of gold. Sabrina is one of the lucky ones with an amazing gift to boot!

The evening started as usual. We were served a warm meal in the soup kitchen at the shelter facility. It was quite yummy I might add! This shelter was primarily for men in a rehab program, but it also had a one room, twelve-bed shelter for women and children in The Fringe. Mind you, these are the *only* twelve beds for women and children in a 100 mile radius. Disturbing information? Yes, I thought so as well.

Even though this is the only shelter for us, it is further disturbing that this is only a night facility. We are not allowed to be here during the day. This is not a women's shelter per say. We must leave each day by 8 a.m., and we are not allowed to show up until 5 p.m. for the evening.

This adds complexities to a woman's life fringing with children. Some of the issues are safety. Some are of basic needs like a bed for a young child to nap during the day. As well, if this facility allowed us to be here during the day we would need child care for our children. Mind you I have not encountered one facility for a woman that does have day care. If they did, we would have better success looking for and obtaining employment. Remember what obstacles I had in searching for employment with a two year old on hand?

Let me get back to Sabrina's story. After eating, we go to the women's dorm room for the evening. We nestle in for the night when our door is locked at 7p.m. for our safety. This is a special time for sharing. We all have our stories to share. We all need fellowship and someone to talk to. Know that being homeless is a rather harsh silent adventure. Communication and connections are elusive to those of us fringing.

So, Sabrina starts sharing her story with me. Tonight is my fifth night at the shelter, it's her first. She broke up with a boyfriend she was staying with, and he kicked her out. She lost her job a few weeks ago, and hasn't been able to get a new one yet. With no cash and no job, it's a trip to the local shelter, maybe for one night or for several. At this point Sabrina says, "I hope my boyfriend will take me back. Then I won't be here long."

This is what is referred to as being "precariously housed." She usually has a place to sleep at night, but it is not her place. She is not able to provide herself secure housing for each night. Most homeless statistics don't even capture this part of the population living in The Fringe Society. She is one of many of them.

For instance, of the children and youth identified as homeless by the Department of Education in FY2000, only 35% lived in shelters; 34% doubled up with family or friends.[7] Now even though

---

7   http://www.nationalhomeless.org/factsheets/who.html

they estimate the children and youth in doubled up, precarious housing, that doesn't estimate those young adults like Sabrina. She is a missing population of the invisible single homeless women in the United States.

So I ask Sabrina, "What kind of job are you looking for?" Her eyes light up with pure joy. "Oh I work with the elderly. I am a caretaker. My mother worked with the elderly that were disabled, and I got my passion for helping them from her." She pauses, thinking, wondering if she should go on, "The last lady I worked for was real nice. She was kind and patient, but had a real bad memory. Alzheimer's they said. We got along great. Her daughter would check on us every couple of days."

She hesitates and proceeds, "I got fired because she didn't like my record keeping on her mom's medications. You see I have my own way of remembering what she had and when. My way is real good and all, but she didn't like it. You see, I can barely read or write." Again she pauses, waiting for my response and probably my judgment and condemnation.

(I mean who wouldn't be concerned if someone couldn't read the instructions on a pill bottle to determine how many and how often? Who wouldn't be concerned if she couldn't keep a written log of what pills she had given and when?)

My only reply is, "That must be really hard." (I know – real genius and thoughtful – right?) She says, "Oh you have no idea. I mean, I can write my name and all. It's just that other daily stuff I don't do in a normal way, but I'm real good at it. I have taught myself how to account for everything I give, and have never made a mistake. But, when the family members find out what I'm doing, they fire me. They don't trust me. I mean I was even working for one family for 3 months. They loved me, they loved my work, and me and my client got along great. My client was responding well to our daily program and routines."

As Sabrina described her work and her clients, I could see she had a rare and beautiful gift for serving the elderly. She shined. She sought to fulfill her destiny and utilize her gifts and talents for the benefit and the good of the world around her. She was a blessing to any of the elderly she worked with. I could see that. There was no question of her talent and her passion.

What a shame that she couldn't have people see past her lack of formal education for her worldly education of taking care of the elderly. If only they weren't so quick to judge. If only they asked questions and engaged in conversation. If only they knew how talented she was! If only they had inquired and listened to her approach and how she handled the daily things like medication… if only…

You and I both know that her lack of basic education is going to be a stumbling block her entire life. She told me she knew she should go back to get her GED. Not as easy as one might think for those fringing. She had the desire, but opportunity escapes her due to constantly changing where she lives and what kind of public transportation she uses and where she lands a job. Being able to go to a community center for GED classes on the north side of town every Wednesday and Saturday from 8-5 for one year isn't real plausible in the life of a Fringe member. (I'm not even sure it's real plausible for someone who isn't a Fringe member—am I right?)

Our lives aren't consistent enough to meld into a seemingly easy schedule to accomplish a simple and necessary goal of obtaining one's GED. Our challenges are many. May Sabrina's story be one for you to pause and wonder what it would be like for someone like her? She is a truly gifted caretaker missing a piece of paper that will validate her as a culturally accepted caretaker.

Our culture doesn't accept or assist those with precarious situations like Sabrina very well. As a matter of fact, our culture continues to judge and shame her for her lack of education and an apparent stereotyping of perceptions of why she can't get her GED. Think of the assumptions that have been made along the way about why she didn't graduate from high school in the first place. BAM! Easy to do, isn't it? I know. I have made the assumptions too. I think pregnancy, perhaps addiction, or maybe gang life. Maybe she ran away as a teenager from a horrible home life of physical abuse. Or maybe she ran away because her family lived with another family and their older child of twenty sexually abused her? Or perhaps she is lazy. Perhaps no one in her life cares if she goes to school or not (it's called a cycle of poverty).

The truth of Sabrina's story, is in a missing awareness, sensitivity and regard for her having to drop out of school early to take care of her own mom when she got cancer. Her passion for caretaking took her out of school and straight to work. But, her passion and gift is being stifled by a piece of paper.

In Sabrina's case many have judged quickly and harshly. Sabrina is a better caretaker than most.

Why is it that we live in a society where athletes can fail school but be rewarded with million dollar contracts for their "natural" abilities but no education? Think it doesn't happen? Oh, it happens all the time! We've all heard of stories of teachers being persuaded to "pass" a student athlete because the school team can't make it without them. There are many athletes who have graduated without earning their diploma.

An uneducated athlete is able to get their job done with their gifts and skills, and Sabrina is also able to get her job done with her gifts and skills. What's one main difference? One got a piece of paper. One didn't. This is food for thought.

While you chew on that (or perhaps you have already spit it out), know that I share Sabrina's secret story in the hope that you may come to consider the assumptions and stereotypes society has dictated about those raised in poverty. Maybe one day you will encounter a Sabrina. I only hope that you won't be so quick to judge her. Maybe you will be inspired to help her. Maybe you will be the one who leads a city crusade to ensure that all women's dorms and shelters have laptops. Maybe you will be the one to come to the shelter twice a week to help her get her online GED?

Sabrina's story is one that should move our thoughts towards the many stuck in a cycle of generational poverty. The fact is that today, almost three-quarters of lower income fourth and eighth graders could not read at grade level in 2013, and over half a million public school students dropped out of grades 9-12 during the 2009-2010 school year.[8] Sabrina is not alone.

Literally society does not want them or know what to do with them. It's overwhelming. What do we do to break the cycle of poverty? How do we give a hand up to those in need? Where does the inspiration and opportunity for a younger generation, in a cycle of poverty, to break free come from?

Perhaps the answer is in you. Provide hope for a child. Change can only happen one person at a time. Magic Johnson says, "All kids need is a little help, a little hope and somebody who believes in them." If only someone had interceded in Sabrina's life when she was a teenager and her mother got cancer. I wonder, did anyone at school call their house to see why she dropped out of school? So easily, scarily, one by one, these children slip through the cracks.

"I've always known I was gifted,
which is not the easiest thing in the world for a person to know,
because you're not responsible for your gift,
only for what you do with it."
– Hazel Scott[9]

---

8   http://www.childrensdefense.org/child-research-data-publications/ state-of-americas-children/documents/2014-SOAC_education.pdf, p. 34
9   http://www.brainyquote.com/quotes/keywords/gifted_3.html

6 ★ Fringe by Death

Some of us in The Fringe are more a member of the secret society by circumstance than choice. Although I know many of you can't understand that. You think, "We all have a choice. You choose to live life as a member of The Fringe. You choose to toddle on the edge of normal, perhaps even enjoy the riskiness of the fight. Somehow fighting to stay just inside the building of *normal*, or just outside of *normal* is exhilarating." I don't debate, that may be true for a few. But for most of us, the shame and stigma of living outside of normal is painful. Looking inside the building, in which we can't seem to catch a break back through that fast revolving door, is disturbing and frustrating.

For some of us, the fight to get back into a normal life has fled. Some have come too far, too fast to even consider going back. I know you can't imagine getting to that point in life. That is why I have to tell you Bud's story.

Bud was a high level police officer. He was a successful detective. He had worked ruthlessly on his way up the ranks to make it to this level of notoriety by age 35. On the way up, he also balanced having a family. He was married and they had three wonderful children.

Bud had come to crack the criminal case of a life time. It was risky, challenging and exhilarating. And as always, he was successful in getting the bad guy.

Only this time was a bit different. The bad guy had deep and dangerous connections in his criminal life and sought revenge against the man who brought him down, Bud.

Fast forward. I met Bud in a soup kitchen. He and I were both regulars. He was a physically intimidating man with great height, a large muscular chest and a confident stature. He emanated power. It was like you could hear the theme song from *The Godfather* playing as he walked by.

We all knew he didn't belong here (not that any of us did). He was a member of The Fringe, but was what we considered on The Fringe of The Fringe. He was an outsider amongst outsiders. Unfortunately even for us in The Fringe, we have our stereotypes too. With Bud, it was like having a homeless Prince William staying and eating at the soup kitchen facility. It was inconceivable that Bud was there.

His modus operandi while there: he didn't speak, he didn't smile. He didn't say thank you to the volunteers serving us. His face showed no emotion. There was no pain. There was no drive. There was no amusement. There was no annoyance. There were only empty eyes staring forward, looking at no one in particular.

What's peculiar is that none of us knew the old Bud. But remnants of his past surrounded him. With all that he had been through, he couldn't shake off his old self. Bud just had that presence about him. The old Bud of initiative, vitality, determination and a wondrous natural instinct for justice was gone. I often wondered about Bud and how he could have such strength and potential, yet just give up. I mean *The Godfather* wouldn't give up. After everything I had been through, I knew I could never give up like that. His destitute attitude was a true mystery to me as it would be to you if you met him.

Then one day, I was told what happened to him. The bastard criminal he put away had Bud's family killed, all of them. He came home and his wife and three children were dead. That was the day that Bud joined The Fringe by death, death of his family, death of his life. In a New York minute the meaning of his life was null and void.

He serves as a vivid example of life gone inconceivably bad. Even though Bud is spiritually null and void, I think he continues to physically live on without his dead wife and children as a way to somehow honor them. Maybe one day the old Bud will surface. Maybe one day he will break through the numbness.

Is his story breaking through your numbness? Bud serves to remind us to not be so quick to judge or condemn any of us fringing. Let this man's suffering and pain be for some good. So, through Bud's story, please remember unless you walk a mile in our shoes, you have no idea what our lives are like.

"When I was a child
I caught a fleeting glimpse
Out of the corner of my eye
I turned to look but it was gone
I cannot put my finger on it now
The child is grown
The dream is gone
And I have become
Comfortably numb."
– Pink Floyd, *The Wall*[10]

---

10   http://www.azlyrics.com/lyrics/pinkfloyd/comfortablynumb.html

7 ★Meeting Ralph

Remember the woman that helped me when I was homeless? She was the woman that would babysit my two year old while I went looking for a job. Well, she also shared her story with me about living in The Fringe. Let's call her FOF Lucy (we'll get to Ralph later in the story). As a matter of fact, I had no idea Lucy was a former secret society member. I was sitting at her dining room table coloring with my son. She was in her forty's, married with two children. Her husband was a businessman and she was a stay at home mom. She was a college graduate with a prestigious work history. They were living a completely normal life in a three bedroom home near the city with two SUVs' and a dog. They were as "normal" as one can get. You could imagine my surprise when Lucy shared her fringing experience with me!

Lucy explained that she has long carried a passion for those with economic hardship. She has a tender spot in her heart for those that have fallen on hard times, like me and my son. She told me that in her early 20's she was periodically homeless. Back then it wasn't called homeless though. In her mind it was described as a time of being mobile, young and free. She never thought of herself as homeless. After all she had her college degree and a decent entry level job in a bank.

But, Lucy didn't have enough money to get her own place. She often wasted her money on clothes, eating out and going out clubbing. Lucy was more of a displaced young adult. She had lived in nine different places in one year.

She lived a few months with mom, a few months with dad, a few months with sister. Then, those welcomes were worn out. She moved in with a friend at work or a sister's friend's house, and another friend's home she worked with. She slept on any couch she could call home for a while. All of her belongings had been pared down to fit into a few Hefty garbage bags.

This mobile and free young woman was fringing. She had to keep moving on. So, since Lucy had fringed, one can see how she would have an aptitude for sensitivity to those currently in The Fringe. The expression, "takes one to know one" comes to mind. That's FOF, Lucy.

So, it is years later when Lucy meets Ralph. She was going about her business. She had to run to a retail store to get something. As she got out of her car, Lucy saw a homeless man sitting on a bench near the store door.

As she walked up towards the retail door, she made eye contact with the man, and was the first to say hello. Those two things, eye contact and speaking to him first are what FOF like to call IDG, or intentional dignity giving.

Lucy had to admit, before she even said hello, she had already wanted to know his story. As luck would have it, he responded to her by saying, "Hello. Excuse me ma'am. Would you mind going down to the grocery store (in the same shopping plaza) and getting me some food? I don't want your money. I don't want to buy alcohol, I just want some beans and weenies and maybe some corned beef hash?" Lucy asked, "What's your name?" He tells her. She responds, "Hi, Ralph."

At this point Lucy is elated! Her heart was beating fast! You see, there was also a great little home style restaurant two doors down in the same plaza. She was thinking just my luck! She then asked, "Ralph, why don't we just go to the restaurant, and I'll buy you a meal and eat with you?"

Lucy so wanted to shower him with a listening ear, kindness and to share a meal with him. She thought maybe he was lonely and would love to have some company to chat with for a while, and maybe even he would share his story with her. Her intentions were to show him some grace and give him back some feeling of belonging, and not being just some stranger or outsider. Little did Lucy know she was getting way ahead of herself thinking that they could become friends and meet once a week to have a meal and talk.

As her heart was pounding and her mind was racing, Ralph's unexpected response came out. "Oh ma'am, that's awfully nice and all. But you see if I eat a good meal like that, and then have to have my next meal from a can; it messes with your head. It would make me realize how good that other food tastes." Lucy felt like she was just shoved backwards by a two ton elephant.

Is that what you would have expected him to say? It certainly wasn't what she expected. She was dumbfounded and didn't have a response. She didn't know what to say other than, "OK, I understand. So, what can I get you at the store?"

He proceeds to tell her a few items he would like, and to make sure they have pop tops, since keeping track of a can opener is difficult. You see, he had all of his belongings in a shopping cart. You can imagine a can opener could easily fall out of the shopping cart holes.

So, off to the store she went. She picked up some beans and weenies, some water, some corned beef hash, and some cookies. Lucy delivered them to him and said good bye. He thanked her with sincere appreciation. She guessed that was all she was supposed to do this time as a friend of The Fringe.

Lucy saw him several more times, each time calling out his name, "Hi, Ralph." IDG – more intentional dignity giving. Maybe she wouldn't ever get to eat a meal with him, but she wanted to still try to give him some sense of belonging in that she knew and remembered his name.

So, if you ever consider working with those in The Fringe, know that there are boundaries, most often set by them. Some may not want any help. Some may want as much as you are willing to give. Some may even take more than what's offered. But as a whole, the members of The Fringe are thoughtful minimalists with contemplative lives.

"The only true boundaries
lie between day and night,
between life and death,
between hope and loss."
— Erin Hunter[11]

11 http://www.goodreads.com/quotes/tag/boundaries

8 ★ Erased from Civilization

The weather is changing. We are moving from late summer into fall. The nights are getting colder. This fact adds many complications. Some hard nights are coming.

Paula lost her home this summer. Till now, Paula has been able to keep it together to at least live in a motel room. But, the end of the month comes. Like her, many cannot afford to pay for the motel room late in the month. Disability and social security checks don't make it far these days. This is when panhandling picks up. It too has a business cycle.

Even with panhandling, my friend, Paula, isn't one of the lucky ones. Not only is she homeless, but now she is shelterless. Tonight Paula sleeps on the streets. It's not like she didn't know it was coming at any moment with the kind of struggles we go through. It's just when it comes, you can't believe the furthering despair and humility. Just when you thought you were nameless, embarrassed, judged, and shamed to a point of complete degradation, more comes.

Even in light of the shame, there are choices to make. Paula's first decision is to consider the park bench or the homeless "camp?" The park bench is risky because of city violations and tickets. It's definitely not a place to get a good few hours of sleep with the harassment from law enforcement. Not that it would deter her from doing it at this point. I mean civilization doesn't understand our motivations or deterrents. She doesn't care about a ticket for she has no money. Can't get blood from a turnip—right?

Option number two is a Fringe homeless camp. This is not an official homeless shelter building. This part of the city where Paula is fringing doesn't have a shelter. She has to resort to true outdoor camping.

There is a beautiful part of the city where Paula lives. It has a long narrow strip of woods set just beside a creek. It is secluded and offers tons of shops and restaurants within minutes of walking. It also bodes many wooded walking trails amongst the trees. It even has a lovely recreational sidewalk nearby for exercise of the concrete sort, like rollerblading or skateboarding or a casual bike ride. It is what city folk would think is a perfect place to camp if described in a "best of KOA" book.

This is not so for us. It is a homeless camp. Many of us find refuge in these parts of the city. I suppose we gather in these outdoor communes because there is safety in numbers. Perhaps someone can explain the psychological need for community, even if one is living in a secret society.

Either way, Paula doesn't make the grade for this option tonight. You see, even in our "community" one has to make the grade. Paula is a newbie to the camp. Spots are limited. Security is tight. Casual drifters are not welcome. So, onward she goes.

Last option for her is near the "best of KOA," under the bridge near the soothing creek. Ah, you may be familiar with the homeless sleeping under bridges. In case you are wondering why, nothing earth shattering; just a good place up in the crevice to protect ourselves from the elements. In Paula's case those elements are quickly approaching, the night with cold temperatures and wind.

She nestles in to the concrete crevice. She uses her backpack as a pillow. Paula holds her purse at her womb like a child would snuggle a stuffed animal. Sleep eventually comes, but at a price. Morning comes. She wakes to find her purse has been stolen.

Now she experiences ultimate humiliation. Paula has no identification now. She is no longer Paula. She is no longer Paula the daughter of, or mother of, or wife of... somehow she has been erased from civilization overnight. She has gone from a woman with a thoughtfully considered birth given name by a loving mother to "Jane Doe."

If she were to die tonight, no one would know who she is. Her mother or her child would never know what happened to her. Paula is erased from the books of civilization.

I expect at this point that there are assumptions being made on how you, a non-fringe member, would handle the situation. Just get up and go get a new ID. But that doesn't work for Paula in The Fringe.

There are many complications. One, no evidence of who she is. There is no file folder at home with a birth certificate or social security card in it. There is no electric bill with her name on it to prove residence. Well, what about the option to obtain a new birth certificate? That might be hard with no mailing address, no money to purchase, and oh—no proof of who you are. Can you imagine?

After about a month, Paula navigates around The Fringe to connect with a center that provides services to obtain a new copy of her birth certificate. Once she has that they will help her get her new ID.

Overall, in a speedy case, it takes over three months to go from erased from civilization, as Jane Doe, back to Paula. That three month's time is like waking up in a different town after an accident with amnesia.

Living on the streets with no identification is the loneliest of places. You are not who you once were. You are Jane Doe. You are a stranger to all. You belong nowhere. No one knows your name. No one knows where you are. No one knows if you are dead or alive.

If you were in a bottomless pit like Paula, what would you do? Where is the answer to getting back to a functioning member of society? Where are the means? What road is mapped out for you? How do you move beyond the despair and shame to become motivated to "get out" of this situation? I wonder if you were erased from civilization, could you handle it without perhaps contemplating suicide? Have you ever felt desperate and trapped in your life? Now take that experience and multiply it by one hundred. How would you fare?

No one living in The Fringe, or anyone else for that matter, deserves the experience of further degradation and invisibility as a human being like Paula went through. If you see those homeless standing on a street corner panhandling for money or food, I hope you come to wonder if they are erased from civilization and that their only proof of existence is the site before your eyes

> *"Being unwanted, unloved, uncared for, forgotten by everybody,*
> *I think that is a much greater hunger,*
> *a much greater poverty than the person who has nothing to eat."*
> – Mother Teresa[12]

---

12   http://www.brainyquote.com/quotes/authors/m/mother_teresa.html

9 ✶ The Hamburger Man

My son and I are sitting in a McDonald's having our lunch. We are sitting against the wall. His back is to the restaurant, and I am looking at the whole restaurant. There is a man sitting kitty-corner to us that I can clearly see. I'll call him the Hamburger Man.

I am attuned to the fact that he may well be a member of The Fringe—not based on stereotypes, but based on my experience. Based on certain locations of places, they have a higher customer base of those in The Fringe. For instance, this McDonald's is in close walking proximity to a few of the "motels" where many homeless families live. The restaurant also happens to tote one of the main bus stops on a key thoroughfare in the city.

So why is he called the Hamburger Man? Well, he sits at his booth having just finished his milkshake. But, he is not the milkshake man. He is the Hamburger Man because under his left hand he holds his coveted hamburger. He doesn't look like he is about to pick it up and eat it. He is just looking, staring off out the window, people watching. Frankly, it looks as if he is saving it for later and protecting his burger from being stolen.

I can relate to that. When there is only one meal a day, it is quite valuable, especially when one doesn't know if there will be enough spare change to get that one meal the next day.

So, I sit and curiously watch. As I sit in my parental time warp while my little one painstakingly, slowly eats his fries, I wonder how long Hamburger Man will wait to eat his hamburger. I would suppose that the shake filled him up, so waiting seems like a good idea to me.

Then, in walks a young Fringe couple and Hamburger Man's face lights up! The couple has smiles on their faces. They have seriously worn shoes with holes, and carry the traditional life essentials in their well worn pillows (or backpacks). They are also carrying their jumbo McDonald's soda cups that this McDonald's allows them to fill daily as a permanent "refill."

Now there is a friend of The Fringe—this McDonald's owner understands his clientele and their needs and helps where he can.

So, the couple walks over to Hamburger Man. He stands up. He hugs them. And then he hands them the hamburger. With lightning speed they open the hamburger, split it in half and gulp their few bites down, all the while still standing. Then they go to the soda machine, fill up and sit down with Hamburger Man to chat.

A short story you say? Yes, it may be a short story, but the significance of this interaction is astounding to me. Now don't freak out, but I'm about to share from my Christian perspective. Just consider me an athlete sharing my experience on how I train for the race. Christianity is the base of my spiritual training—'nough said.

Hamburger Man's story brings to mind the story of a widow woman in the Bible that gave only two copper coins when the plate was passed. Everyone around her gave their fair share, but she gave only a few cents. It seemed small, insignificant. She may even have been considered greedy by others because she gave so little.

The unexpected twist of this Bible story goes like this, "Jesus said, "Truly I tell you, this poor widow has put more into the treasury than all the others. They all gave out of their wealth; but she, out of her poverty, put in everything—all she had to live on." That's from the book of Mark, Chapter 12 verse 43 and 44.

Hamburger Man, it is an honor to know you. You have a heart of gold. You are a truly selfless person in a selfish world. You are compassion. You are inspiration. Your heart, your life in The Fringe, your overwhelming generosity of giving what little you had, it speaks to what I cannot say. You are a perfect example of what others need to know through your story, dear Hamburger Man!

> *"No thoughtful man ever came to the end of his life,*
> *and had time and a little space of calm from which to look back upon it,*
> *who did not know and acknowledge that it was what he had done unselfishly and for others,*
> *and nothing else, that satisfied him in the retrospect,*
> *and made him feel that he had played the man."*
> – Woodrow Wilson[13]

---

13   http://www.quoteland.com/author/Woodrow-Wilson-Quotes/1753/?pg=2

10 CHRISTMAS IN SEPTEMBER

I t's September. It's that time of year in Florida for the annual Stand Down. For those not in The Fringe Society, let me explain. This is a special one day county wide event put on by the National Coalition for Homeless Veteran's. Many cities across the country have them.

The original Stand Down for homeless veterans was modeled after the Stand Down concept used during the Vietnam War to provide a safe retreat for units returning from combat operations. At secure base camp areas, troops were able to take care of personal hygiene, get clean uniforms, enjoy warm meals, receive medical and dental care, mail and receive letters, and enjoy the camaraderie of friends in a safe environment. Stand Down afforded battle-weary soldiers the opportunity to renew their spirit, health and overall sense of well-being. That is the purpose of the Stand Down for homeless veterans, and achieving those objectives requires a wide range of support services and time.[14]

So this Stand Down is put together by many social services on behalf of assisting the local homeless, with a major focus on services for the veterans. All of these services are offered in one location for the day, instead of the usual fifteen different places.

---

14   http://nchv.org/index.php/service/service/stand_down/

Some of these services include: podiatry services, dental services, flu shots, food stamp filing, disability filings with Social Security, showers, toiletry bags, a hot meal, free haircuts and others. The fact that all of these services are centrally located for the day brings unusual convenience to members of The Fringe.

At this VA Stand Down, they even offered free services to meet with a local judge to clear misdemeanors from their record. Many of these misdemeanor charges are a part of life for those fringing. It might be a ticket for public loitering (sleeping in public), or for panhandling, or worse for indecent exposure (urinating in a public park and getting caught). Money to pay for these tickets isn't a likely luxury. But these tickets stay on the books bogging down local court systems with tracking and monitoring. So, this service is offered as a win win for all to resolve these outstanding issues.

Many Friends of The Fringe are here helping. Some serve meals, some escort clients to each section of the services. One of the FOF is a woman in her 40's. She is assisting clients waiting to see the judge. She is surprised by their respect and reverence for the judge. One man claims he isn't ready see the judge and that someone else can take his turn. He is yet waiting for a toiletry bag so he can shave at the water fountain before seeing the judge.

Can you imagine? Not what you expected? He is not feeling entitled. He is not feeling slighted or owed. He is not obtuse to manners or etiquette or respect for the judge. He is a forgotten, fallen war hero with blisters on his feet from wet socks and ill fitting free shoes. He has a sun weathered face with kind smile lines, yet eyes of deep pain and loss. Or perhaps it's not loss, but just plain mental anguish from life in The Fringe.

He is perhaps a token "poster child" of the homeless, as 40% of homeless men have served in the armed forces.[15]

Near and beyond the "poster child" veteran waiting for the judge, there is another commotion going on. There is a new se-

---

15   http://www.nationalhomeless.org/factsheets/who.html

niors' facility opening up that needs workers. Word has spread fast. They need to find two men that can provide maintenance for the residents. In exchange for their services to maintain the property, they will each be given their own room to live in for free with meals included. That is like winning the lottery for many of these men in need of employment and housing.

How does one go about interviewing or selecting the right men for the job? Well, not by normal standards. FOF know most of these homeless in the community from daily contact in one way or another for friendship or assistance or a hot meal. They aren't invisible to everyone. So, the owners of the new facility ask the "Boss FOF" about potential men to fill the two spots.

Boss FOF knows, and at this point it pays to know Boss FOF. She calls out two young men's names. They come to the front to talk with Boss FOF. The two young men are brothers. Both had previously been in the construction business for decades. They were part of the recessionary impact on the Gulf Coast after the BP oil spill of 2007. Construction work became a thing of the past. Many of the current homeless in this area were former construction workers.

Boss FOF says, "These are your boys. They are healthy, sober and hard working. They have found hard times and could use a break." Based on her hearty recommendation and knowledge of these young men, they are welcomed to join them at the new facility. The two brothers hug each other and hug Boss FOF. There are tears streaming, no make that pouring down their faces like Hawaiian waterfalls. That is something one doesn't see every day, pure joy, pure relief. They were getting a ticket out of The Fringe. It was Christmas in September!

I was thinking it couldn't get any better than this, when I heard more. Not only were they going to live for free at the facility, but they would not have to work full time since it was a new facility. The time they had, they could use to look for a full time job.

Ah, you say, well they should have been looking for full time work all the while. Don't worry, they were. But one's line of work and employment is limited with challenges unbeknownst to those not in The Fringe. The most oppressive challenge; no address and phone number for the application to get an interview or a call. Now they would have a real address to put on their applications, and a real home phone number to receive messages and phone calls about going on interviews and securing employment.

This was a huge step forward in gaining back their identity, dignity and self respect. Watching those two young men was something I will never forget. Also watching the faces of those that didn't get one of the spots was something else I will never forget. Fear, disappointment, another let down, "a break for someone else, why not me?," another cold lead, another cold night....they hang their heads low and turn around and go back to whatever line they were in.

One might wonder whether those left behind were inspired with hope that they might get their chance next time. Or, that it was the nail in the coffin that cut off their last bit of hope in a long line of let downs in a complicated and lonely life that chipped out the last bit of dignity in themselves.

> *"Life is not a matter of place, things or comfort;*
> *rather, it concerns the basic human rights of family, country,*
> *justice and human dignity."*
> – Imelda Marcos[16]

---

16   http://www.brainyquote.com/quotes/keywords/human_dignity.html

11 ⋆ The Holiday Riddle

The holiday season brings to light so many opportunities to help those less fortunate. For instance, the Salvation Army bells are ringing, many adopt a family for Christmas, and there is a huge spike in volunteers at soup kitchens across the country on Thanksgiving and Christmas Day. It is a time of year when the "fortunate" ones realize and are thankful for the many blessings they have. So, they too as friends of The Fringe reach out in extra earnest during the holidays to show support and care and love for unbeknownst members of the secret society, The Fringe.

The holiday season comes and goes for those in The Fringe just like it does for everyone else. You know how it goes, lights go up, tree goes up, and meals are cooked. Meals are eaten. Family goes home. Tree comes down. Lights come down. All is boxed till next year.

However, the love showered on those in The Fringe during the holidays isn't soon forgotten, believe you me! My son still clutches to his favorite teddy bear that was given to him when we were on the run and homeless.

Let's take a glimpse into the lives of a family during the holidays that are fringing. Other than where they live being different, their lives are much like everyone else's. This family has a mom and dad and a nine year old son. He goes to school every day, just like all of the other kids. The son is a bright, delightful 3rd grader! He is well known in his school, having been only one of eight out of grades K-8 to receive an award as "Outstanding Citizen" by a local club that year.

It was public knowledge in this community about the economic hardships this family faced. The community had watched as the situation worsened. They used to live in the neighborhood where the school is, but were evicted and now live in a motel. If you could have seen the horror of what they went through on eviction, you would be repulsed. They lived on the fringe for a year before eviction. As eviction came closer, they couldn't do much but wait. Neither parent had a job. No job, no lease. No lease, no home.

I beseech that poetic pause again. Think about it. No job..... no lease. Please don't just read the words, think about them. These simple phrases I write to bring perspective are simple in words, but deep in ramifications. Who would lease to someone with no income, even if they could make a deposit? No lease...no home. Not having a job is probably more complicating to their lives than one can imagine.

Anticipating with great apprehension of eviction, the best this family could hope for would be to put their belongings in storage and get them out later. But even that option is riddled with complications. Moving a house full of belongings into storage requires a truck and lots of man hours. Their van isn't going to cut it. A truck costs money they don't have. And, of course the storage unit costs money as well, which they have none of. That would eliminate the storage option.

The day came. The police show up with the eviction notice to immediately vacate the premises. They leave, that in and of itself is disheartening, to have to leave your home, your memories and your family heirlooms behind. But what happened next is utterly devastating, devaluing, disturbing, demoralizing and injurious. Other than the items loaded into their van, all of their belongings were then thrown out. Oh we are not talking about items being thrown into a large trash receptacle. We are not talking about all of their memories and heirlooms being hauled away for donation sales. We are talking about the cruelty of heaping all of their belongings into a huge pile on their former front lawn.

Never has one seen something so disgraceful. It not only was embarrassing for them, but demonstrated pure disregard for the whole neighborhood. Their family heirlooms were heaped, strewn and broken. It wasn't even confined to the front yard. There was broken glass, dishes, lamps and mirrors all over the yard, the sidewalk, and down to the street.

(This is their actual home in Mysterytown, USA)

Mind you, the "bank" who took possession didn't have new owners. No one was moving in. It would be months before the house went to auction. It would be even longer before someone would renovate and move in. So, why would they do such a thing? Couldn't they just evict the family and leave them some dignity for the moment without such unnecessary cruelty? This was truly a heinous act of malicious proportions. This child still had to go to school in this neighborhood. Can you imagine the shame?

I digress. So, where were we? Oh, back to the move. The family moved into a nearby motel. This motel was almost 100% occupied by other homeless families. I know, you can't believe there are such whole communities like this for those of us fringing.

National statistics show that 23% of homeless people live in motels.[17] Odd jobs, sporadic income and hotel vouchers from churches and other organizations allow these families to live in these motels.

So, the family is about six months along in their homelessness. As mentioned, luckily the 3rd grader was close enough to still attend the same school. Most days the car worked well enough to get him there, sometimes it didn't. He still had play dates with his friends, only they didn't come to his "house" to play. And he didn't have sleepovers at his house. He was being secluded in small but material ways from *normal* society.

Because of their hardships, the friends of The Fringe, who awarded the outstanding child, had this family on their radar to help them during the holidays.

So, it was arranged to bring a holiday meal basket to the family. The plan was to deliver it early so that the family wouldn't have to worry about the upcoming meal on the special holiday. The basket was brought to them about a week before the holiday. The basket was overflowing with goodies, fresh fruits and vegetables, sweets and desserts and the prized holiday turkey with all the trimmings! Poetic pause, if I may?

So, think of this as a holiday riddle. What's wrong with this picture? Okay, inherently besides the fact that a family with a young child is homeless, what else? Before I expound on my perception of what's wrong, let me set your heart in the right direction. A man once said, "Don't just meet the needs, meet the people with the needs." WOW... say it with me, "Don't just meet the needs, meet the people with the needs."

Yes, it was a wonderful gesture of the FOF to remember this family with a young child during the holidays. Gathering and de-

---

17   http://www.nationalhomeless.org/factsheets/who.html

livering this bountiful meal, that is a beautiful thing. I don't want to distract from the good deed, but there is a lesson in this story for you.

If one doesn't become engaged in the everyday lives of those they hope to serve, how can one honor them and serve them? A basic understanding of the lives of those we intend to help is not only helpful in moving towards efficiency in advancing their success to self-sufficiency, but it is required.

So, I ask, what if ... what if FOF didn't just deliver the holiday meal, but asked them to join *them* for the holiday meal? Put up a flyer at the motel and give a date and time when you will be delivering a holiday meal. Have a pot luck prepared with some of your neighbors. Bring in some folding tables and chairs. Set up in the parking lot or on the lawn near the motel and break out the bountiful cooked meal. You could even get crazy and play Christmas music and bring one small stuffed animal for each person. Sit with them, eat with them, talk with them, laugh with them.

In the course of actually sharing a meal, time, music and conversation is when the layers of the onion are peeled back to reveal some of the challenges of being a homeless family in fringing.

So, where was I? I digress as usual. This is where I wish to dispel some of the mysteries of our lives in The Fringe. So, how many of you have figured out the holiday riddle?

The answer to the riddle is that in the lives of the homeless family, in particular for this family, you will come to realize that there is no refrigerator to store the turkey for a week. It is a one room motel room. The "kitchen" is a small table in the corner with a toaster oven and a microwave, and no refrigerator.

Not only is there no refrigerator, there is another challenge for this family living in secrecy. Even if they could store the turkey and the trimmings for a week in a fridge, where would they cook it? This is a motel. There is no oven, and a toaster oven doesn't cut it.

What the friends of The Fringe did for the family was a wonderful outreach! The family found dignity, honor and delight in being remembered.

Have no worries, the food didn't go to waste. Members of The Fringe are resourceful. They fired up the barbie and grilled the turkey that day.

"I hear and I forget. I see and I remember.
I do and I understand."
— Confucius[18]

---

18   http://www.brainyquote.com/quotes/keywords/remember.html

12 The Avid Reader

I am in yet another soup kitchen. This one serves about 300 meals, three times a day. That's almost a 1,000 mouths fed every day. Some are very regular customers—based on proximity to the kitchen and where a Fringe member is "living" (if one can call it that). At this table is a young man I have seen several times before.

He is probably in his early twenties. He is about five foot eight and weighs in at about 250 pounds. His hair is light brown and he has a gentle demeanor. Some others aren't so sweet in demeanor. Some are so angry and mad that they will let you know up front to not even look at them. Body language and facial expressions are key forms of communication in The Fringe. But this young man seems optimistic, kind and comfortable with where he is.

Not only did I sense his gentle demeanor, but one of the FOF does as well. She is serving us in the soup kitchen. Her job is to chat us up and make us feel welcome during our meal. She walks over and asks us, "Can I get ya'll some more water?"

"Why yes," he responds, all the while his eyes stay pinned to his book that he is engrossed reading.

She grabs his mug and fills it full with ice cold water. As she sets it down, she leans inward over his shoulder and asks him, "What book are you reading?" Bewildered, he thinks, *"Are you talking to me?"* Befuddled, he looks up and tells her the name of the book. She responds, "Oh, who is the author?" He proceeds to flip to the front of the book and shows her the author's name. As well, he directs her attention to the inside page that lists all of the author's books.

They exchange a few more lines of conversation about the author and what types of books he writes. The FOF gets out a piece of paper and writes down the author's name so she can get one of the books at the library. He provides advice on which book is best to start with. "Sounds good," she says. "Thank you for sharing with me."

Now, beyond baffled, he looks up, smiles and utters with astonishment, "Sure, no problem."

Before the interaction concludes, he looks up, smiles again and asks, "Why did you ask me what I was reading?"

"I was curious."

His question may have been verbalized as, "Why did you ask me what I was reading?" But, the real meaning behind his question was, "*Why did she see me? Why wasn't I invisible? Why you and why now?*"

So, what is the true meaning to share behind this Fringe encounter? Well, the initial question seems simple enough, right? "What are you reading?" Yet that simple question was one this young man hadn't been asked in several months. He was an avid reader with his nose always stuck in a book. Not only was he an avid reader, but he was an invisible member of The Fringe Society.

Perhaps within this story is a perfect example that *normal* society really hasn't been attuned to our existence among them and therefore cannot help but not see what is invisible. Perhaps the Avid Reader was ashamed of his existence in the Fringe and hoped to hide behind his book, even in that soup kitchen where there were 300 of us. I suppose his book was his mask. I am suggesting that maybe he even wanted to be invisible.

Even in the Fringe Society, no one paid much attention to him. No one spoke to him. No one asked him what book he was reading, and certainly no one cared who the author was and what his suggestions for reading were. He was invisible among the invisibles. But mind you, perhaps our reasons for not acknowledging him are probably very different. When you are living in the Fringe and dying on the inside a little more every moment, withering in hope and shamed of a lack of normal existence, books are not often within our train of thoughts. Most of us fringing really don't care what book he is reading. The angst of our life fringing demands full attention, and hobbies such as reading aren't normally a priority.

So, back to the question she asked, "What are you reading?" That simple interaction gave him dignity. It gave him belonging and importance and a feeling of significance in a lonely world, a feeling he hadn't felt in a really long time. It was as simple as the fact that someone cared enough to just ask..."What are you reading?"

Never underestimate the power of inquiry. One never knows what that interaction really meant to him. But in that moment, I saw his puzzlement and his bewilderment over a simple question. I saw the space of his soul span out a bit further as they engaged in this conversation. I saw a man who finally felt significant yet again, if only for a fleeting moment.

My hope is that after reading our stories in *The Fringe*, blinders will be removed, whether it is fear or disgust or ignorance that hinders others from seeing us and perhaps even talking to us.

Then and only then might others, besides FOF, not be afraid to ask a simple question of a lonely stranger. Members of The Fringe are not invisible, so please be stirred to quit living as if we are.

"Sometimes the heart sees what is invisible to the eye."
– H. Jackson Brown, Jr.[19]

---

19   http://www.brainyquote.com/quotes/keywords/invisible.html

13 CATCH-22

The phrase "Catch-22," "a problematic situation for which the only solution is denied by a circumstance inherent in the problem or by a rule,"[20] had entered the English language[21] via the satirical novel titled the same and written by Joseph Heller. The phrase Catch-22 also enters into the language and life of those fringing.

There is a woman in The Fringe named "Charlotte." She is a smart and resourceful woman. By smart I don't only mean street smart or book smart or people smart, but overall highly intelligent. It is apparent to all who meet her. Her intelligence gives her a bit of a competitive edge in life despite her becoming a member of our secret society of shame. She is determined to use those gifts to figure out a way to get out of this secret society.

Her story isn't about how she became a member of The Fringe. Charlotte's story is about how she is trapped in our secret society, despite her high intelligence and resourcefulness. She is much like our friend Bud. Remember Bud, *The Godfather* from Chapter 6? He was a member of The Fringe, but was considered on the fringe of The Fringe. Well, Charlotte is also like that. There is something about her with this gifted intelligence and that gleam in her eye that puts her on the fringe of The Fringe. She is a misfit among misfits, like Rudolph in the land of misfit toys.

---

20   Catch-22. 2012. In Merriam-Webster.com. Retrieved March 8, 2012, from http://www.merriam-webster.com/dictionary/catch%2022

21   http://en.wikipedia.org/wiki/Catch-22

In the way of her gifts she may be among the elite and the few, but she also has a common denominator with many in The Fringe. She is one among the 38% of the homeless that suffers from addiction.[22]

OK, sidebar alert! Your pulse is racing—you wondered when I would get to a story about "that" kind of homeless person. I take it you are very familiar with this type of homeless person. You think, "Yeah, I know all about them. They stand on the street corners begging for money which they will only use for their next bottle. And that's why I refuse to help those standing on street corners begging for money."

Well, that is OK. You are entitled to your opinion. I don't and won't judge you for your decision about whether to give money to those strangers on the street corner or not. But, I must challenge your opinion. So, one must ask, what assumptions are your opinions based on?

Let's call these assumptions for what they are. They are simply stereotypes. We are back to the bad apple. There are stereotypes of the homeless, and often those stereotypes impact one's perception of *all* homeless people. And yes, while not all homeless people have addiction problems, there is a whopping 38% that do.

Therefore, out of my duty to help enlighten *normal* society on members of The Fringe, I have to share the story of Charlotte. All I am asking is that before you jump to conclusions on those in The Fringe, especially with addiction problems; please walk a mile in their shoes with me.

This will not be an easy mile. You know in the story of *The Christmas Carol* when there are the three tours given by the ghosts of Christmas Past, Present and Future. Well, this tour will be much like the last tour given by the Grim Reaper of Christmas Future in *The Christmas Carol.*

---

22 http://www.nationalhomeless.org/factsheets/who.html

As one might expect being guided by the Grim Reaper, the journey would be bleak, dark and depressing. But no worries, we'll leave ol' Reaper out of it. I will be your guide and promise to deliver you safely back to the present. Come with me.

Charlotte has struggled with addiction issues for most of her life. She was dropped off (disposed of by her mom like a pizza delivery) at her grandmother's house to live where other cousins were "delivered." Some of them were older and exposed her to their world. She started using marijuana and alcohol at age thirteen.

She soon ran away after someone tried to abuse her. She used other drugs in her life including battling an addiction to crack. She actually beat her addition to crack while in jail serving time for possession of said drug and intent to sell.

She is in her forties at this point. She is an alcoholic, no longer using marijuana. She has lost everything. She is homeless. She has even lost custody of her son as a result of domestic complications with her addiction issues.

So one might think if she was determined enough, she should just go get sober and get on with her life? Pick up the pieces and then get a job. Right? This is exactly what she was thinking. Charlotte entered detox, not once, not twice, not three times, but seven times.

Entering detox takes a humiliating posture for anyone, fringing or not. There is admittance to failure, but a yielding to start a road to recovery and a rebuilding of self esteem. The problem starts after Charlotte is released from detox. The next step so that she is able to empower herself to beat her addiction is to enter a rehabilitation program. This is a most precarious situation for those fringing. This is where it gets complicated.

In order for her to get into a rehab program for women, there is a six week waiting list. Six weeks! Six weeks of sobriety in a world of shame, neglect, fear and common drug use is like 1,000 years in hell.

After all seven times of detox comes the real struggle as one can imagine, or can one? Those six weeks of sobriety while fringing and waiting is a fine line between life and death—seriously. She doesn't really have a choice but to do it on her own. She doesn't have the same opportunity as normal society to enter rehab upon release from detox. She isn't able to pay for her rehab program or to have insurance cover her rehab. Charlotte has to wait on a long list for a program that is specifically funded to help those that cannot pay for rehab.

It gets more complicated. On one of her stints of sobriety I got to know her. She honestly tried to carry on in the streets and to hang in there until there was an opening at the rehab center. While waiting for her opening at the rehab center, she had fallen off the radar. She is one of the victims that had her purse stolen while sleeping. In it was her only link to society as a whole, her ID. She is like Paula, in Chapter 8, who was erased from civilization overnight.

Charlotte has now also gone from a woman with a thoughtfully considered birth given name by a loving mother to "Jane Doe." Timing can be everything in this life and death situation. Yes, her spot came open at rehab and while she was still sober. Only she was sober Jane Doe. She was still in her waiting period to obtain her reissued ID. No Jane Doe is allowed in any rehab program, even if an opening comes up. Charlotte was passed by for the next person on the list.

As you can guess, she lost her sobriety before she could get her new ID, get back on the list and get into rehab.

On yet another cycle of sobriety, Charlotte had plugged into an outpatient program while waiting for an inpatient program to open up a spot for her again. She was to attend meetings three times a week from 6-9 p.m. BAM! There it is, the Catch-22. She can't attend the meetings. Why? Good question, keep asking questions. One might think she has nothing else to do, so why can't she? What excuse does she come up with?

Have you ever heard of the lottery? This isn't the state lottery or a scratch off game of any kind. This is the homeless shelter lottery. How does it work? Well, those needing shelter for the night stand in line for hours in the morning for a turn to walk up and receive a lottery token for the day.

Those lucky enough to receive a token before the shelter runs out of them will have a place to sleep that evening. If you are one of the lucky ones to win the shelter lottery, you then go back to the streets for the day to wait for the 7 p.m. check in. Charlotte was often one of the lucky ones winning the lottery.

Now she has a tough decision to make. Will she attend the outpatient drug treatment meeting from 6-9 p.m., or will she make curfew and be at the shelter by 7 p.m. for a place to sleep that night where she won a token? She can't do both. She has to decide whether to go to a meeting for three hours and then sleep on the street, or go to the shelter to be safe and warm for the night in these winter months.

This is a perfect description of a Catch-22, "a problematic situation for which the only solution is denied by a circumstance inherent in the problem or by a rule,[23]"

After having missed three of the meetings, she is cut from the program. Her name is removed from the wait list. Charlotte is yet again back to struggling with a life-long addiction on her own. She is further humiliated, condemned and knocked back down. There is no dignity to be found in failing yet again.

She is a prime example of what the National Coalition for the Homeless describes in their account of the relationship between homelessness and substance abuse.

> Substance abuse is often a cause of homelessness. Addictive disorders disrupt relationships with family and friends and often cause people to lose their jobs. For

---

23 Catch-22. 2012. In Merriam-Webster.com. Retrieved March 8, 2012, from http://www.merriam-webster.com/dictionary/catch%2022

people who are already struggling to pay their bills, the onset or exacerbation of an addiction may cause them to lose their housing. According to Didenko and Pankratz (2007), two-thirds of homeless people report that drugs and/or alcohol were a major reason for their becoming homeless.

In many situations, however, substance abuse is a result of homelessness rather than a cause. People who are homeless often turn to drugs and alcohol to cope with their situations. They use substances in an attempt to attain temporary relief from their problems. In reality, however, substance dependence only exacerbates their problems and decreases their ability to achieve employment stability and get off the streets. Additionally, some people may view drug and alcohol use as necessary to be accepted among the homeless community (Didenko and Pankratz, 2007).

Breaking an addiction is difficult for anyone, especially for substance abusers who are homeless. To begin with, motivation to stop using substances may be poor. For many homeless people, survival is more important than personal growth and development, and finding food and shelter take a higher priority than drug counseling. Many homeless people have also become estranged from their families and friends. Without a social support network, recovering from a substance addiction is very difficult. Even if they do break their addictions, homeless people may have difficulty remaining sober while living on the streets where substances are so widely used (Fisher and Roget, 2009). Unfortunately, many treatment programs focus on abstinence only programming, which is less effective than harm-reduction strategies and does not address the possibility of relapse (National Health Care for the Homeless Council, 2007).[24]

So, before one judges those that are homeless and may have substance abuse problems, consider their plight. They don't need condemnation, but help and understanding for a future with hope.

Charlotte's failure to be adequately equipped to fight and conquer her addiction feeds her self-loathing, exasperation, frustration, desperation and anger. I have seen her cry hysterically. She wants to beat her addiction. She wants out of The Fringe more than you know. She wants her life back. She wants her son back. But this homelessness puts her in the corner of a crafty, shrewd and cunning maze with seemingly no way out.

That, my friends, is a Catch-22.

"But what we call our despair is often only the painful eagerness of unfed hope."
– George Eliot

---

24   http://www.nationalhomeless.org/factsheets/addiction.html

14 CHILDREN OF THE FRINGE

I am scared. I am fretful. I am intimidated by the thought of having to share with you about the youngest members of our secret society, but it is time to break their silence.

It is in our nature to protect our children. It is in our nature to deny the devastating impact that our lives in The Fringe have on our children. It brings with it emotionally charged feelings that "I am a failure as a parent." Some might even think I should have my son taken from me because of fringing. Hold on before you agree so readily. I am ashamed and embarrassed enough.

I am keenly astute to the fact that no person, let alone a child should have to experience the stress, humiliation, and state of flummox of living fringing. Our lives are riddled with inconsistency, tentativeness, uncertainty, trepidation and anxiety. But our youth aren't able to articulate those feelings. They aren't emotionally mature enough to verbalize those things. For they have a completely different perspective on what life is like in The Fringe. So, it is time to share their story, through their eyes.

This may be the first time you have ever heard about what life is like for a homeless child, but I can guarantee it won't be the last time. National attention has just been raised on our plight. New statistics in late 2014 have come out that are shocking America. "1 in 30 children in America are homeless. That equates to **2.5 million children** that are homeless in America." [25]

---

25   http://new.homelesschildrenamerica.org/mediadocs/275.pdf (page 1, November 27, 2014)

Perspective please! If the average school class size across the country is 30 students, what kind of impact are we talking about? That means that in every state, in every city, in every school, in every class room there is a homeless child amongst them.

That is not a national statistic to be proud of. But that is the reality of poverty in America. Maybe now that the children are involved, people will take notice of this secret society, The Fringe. Now is the time to read on and set aside judgment and preconceived notions of how and who the poor are in this great country we live in. These homeless children, one in every classroom, are our future.

Ella is one of those children. She is a homeless teenager. As you can imagine like any teen, getting them to talk is a nightmare. They don't want to be bothered with such brain activities as being insightful, introspective or revealing of their teen lives. It wastes energy needed for cultivating attitude, and it interrupts vegging out (code for contemplative teen thoughts of nothingness amongst selfies). Besides all that, they dread talking to adults because adults are notoriously stupid.

Now, compound all the privacy needs and inherent mystery of teen life with that of a fringing teen and you have the recipe, if for nothing else, a gripping story.

Ella's perspective is one of a girl in her early teen years. Her bio alone is revealing of fringe living as unpredictable, ever changing and tenuous. She has spent half of her life growing up in The Fringe. She has lived in four different states. She has been in foster care in two different homes. She's been reunited with her family both times. In recent years, she has lived mostly in motels (four that I know of). In addition, she has changed schools the last three consecutive years.

Now if I may, let me give you a visual to set the stage for you. Most have seen the movie *Charlie and the Chocolate Factory*. In the first part of the movie there is a scene where we get a glimpse into Charlie Bucket's life. He arrives at his humble home. The scene shows that he lives with his mom and dad and his four elderly grandparents. These seven people are living in what is a one room house. This small house has only one bed. Comically (or not) there are four elderly grandparents, all in the one bed. Charlie and his parents sleep on an additional mattress on the floor. His mom is cooking and serving cabbage soup for dinner, after having it for lunch, yet again.

That is much of what Ella's real life looks like. Unfortunately, Ella has yet to receive her golden ticket to get out of poverty, like Charlie Bucket did.

As I asked Ella to share her story with you and I, no shock for a teenager, she really didn't want to talk about it, but agreed to write it all down. So, here is Ella's story, out of the mouth of a babe:

> I may only be a young teenager, but people always tell me how mature I am for my age. I don't think they mean mature as in grown up, but mature as in "experienced." That is the first thing you will notice or learn about homeless children. We live with the exposure, knowledge and experience of an adult. We are robbed of our childhood, only we don't really realize it. It's normal for us.
>
> One day I realized how different my life was from other kids. There were four of us playing together for an entire day. Two kids were FOF, and two of us homeless. We were hanging at their FOF house for the day. At the end of the day when I was being driven back to my motel, I realized that was the *first* time I actually felt like a real kid. I had not a care in the world. I knew where my next meal was coming from as I soaked up the smells of a home-cooked meal. I laughed all day. I was so happy. I was worry free. I was content. I felt peaceful. I will never forget those feelings. They provide me with grit to get through on many others.

But, as I am being driven back to my world… I am very sad. It took these stark realities to make me finally realize just how much I want to be a normal kid. I don't know how to explain it, but my world is just not that fun. It's depressing. It's hard. It stinks.

There are lots of reasons it stinks. What do I want you to know? Well, I have never had a play room. I have never had a bunch of toys. Not that those are really important. But they would be nice to have. If you think about motel living, we don't even have a couch, or an oven or a washer and dryer. I don't even have four pairs of socks. I don't have a favorite stuffed animal. We only have our basics that must fit into two back packs each. A stuffed animal is a luxury that doesn't fit – literally. I don't have a pet. You have no idea how much I want a dog or cat!

When I lived in a house before we lived in motels, we didn't have heat. We had a wood burning stove in the one room where we all slept to keep us warm. We didn't have electricity, so to have a hot bath my mom heated a bunch of pots of water on the gas stove to pour into the tub to make it almost warm for a bath.

So, coming from that, living in a motel seems to be a step up for us. At least we have a shower and hot water and heat in the winter! But there are still many worries for us even though we have a place to stay. The only thing for sure in my life is worry.

I don't know where my next meal is coming from. I don't know if I will have a place to sleep at night. The end of the month comes and all my mom talks about is that we have to beg on a street corner because our money is gone. We don't have enough to pay our motel bill. So for every day during that last week of the month, my parents are all stressed out and argue a lot. I can't stand it.

Most often we get through with begging or with vouchers from churches.

That is the week, every month, when my long bus ride home is super stressful. I hate it. As I get closer to my stop, I get sick to my stomach. One time to my complete embarrassment, I actually got so stressed out that I puked on the bus. What I'm afraid of is that my parents are going to be at the bus stop with our back packs, which means we have no place to sleep.

If I am not worried about Back Pack Bus Stop Day, I live in fear of being taken away or separated from my family. Two times the cops have come and taken me away. One time I got to go back home after three weeks. The other time, I didn't get to live with my mom until almost a year later. I never know if the cops will come to take me away again.

There was another time when my mom got put in jail for six weeks for violating her probation. Somehow, luckily they didn't take me into foster care. I think the cops who picked her up didn't realize she had a kid. I had to fend for myself, nothing new really. Luckily my mom was dating a guy and I got to stay with him until my mom got out.

In one of the schools I went to before we lived in motels, I was the *only* one who was poor (no I'm not exaggerating or kidding). Everyone knew we had nothing. Lots of people helped us and gave us things for Christmas.

Once I was in the school counselor's office. She called another school parent to ask for help to buy me new shoes when they noticed mine had holes in them. I was so embarrassed. I mean who cares if my shoes have holes in them. Do they make a difference in how I learn or what grade I get? No they don't. I am getting all A's and B's. So why are they so focused on my shoes? I don't understand. All I know is that I am singled out and different. There is so much attention on me because we are poor. It makes me really uncomfortable.

To sum it up, uncomfortable is a good overall description of what my life is like in The Fringe. That and awkward. That's really about all I can say. I don't know what else normal people should know about living in The Fringe.

As I read what Ella wrote to share with us, I was dumbstruck by her lack of emotion and the way she stated her life as matter of fact. She compartmentalizes well. Her perspective is honest and raw. But there is so much more that I know about her that I want to share with you. I need to go deeper. I have to find the guts to tell you some disturbing realities of her life.

One of the most impactful realities of her homeless teen life is that she doesn't know what privacy is. Like Charlie in *Charlie and the Chocolate Factory*, she shares a one room motel with two and sometimes three family members. In her home prior to motel living, it was the same conditions as Charlie; they all slept in one room where the wood stove was. She is rarely alone, and I don't mean from a good parenting stand point of supervision.

In my experience, this close quarter's living environment inhibits her growth towards self sufficiency. It establishes her need to have someone near her at all times. "People proximity" is one of the learned traits of fringing. It's a homeless child's legacy.

How does this behavior translate to the non-fringing world? On the rare occasion when visiting non-fringing friends, she cannot leave their side. Literally, if a friend goes to the bathroom, she will camp just outside the door on the floor to wait for them to come out.

Now I am no social behavioral expert, and have no proof of what I'm about to say, but it seems to me that this crisis of proximity developed in childhood of impoverished kids will have and has had a direct impact on their choices as adolescents and as adults.

Based on that idea, dare I say that perhaps it is because of this overwhelming need for "people proximity" that influences those raised in poverty to engage early in sexual relationships and results in higher teen pregnancy rates. It is well known, documented, studied and published that teenage pregnancy is more common among the poor in our country. "People proximity," a self proclaimed label by me, is one for some social scientist to chew on for new research.

Sorry I digress (again). Let's move on from here. Let me just say that even though Ella is never alone, she is rarely engaged in her environment. Isolation is a way of life. Little speech is spoken. Ella rarely gets invited to hang out with other kids since she no longer lives in a neighborhood with other classmates. She has a long public transit bus ride to school each morning. Another major part of teen life is socialization via sleepovers. She can't have any sleep over's at her motel, the shame of her living conditions prohibits it.

The isolation deepens still. Ella doesn't have involvement in after school sports. She isn't the only one. None of the kids living in their motel are involved in sports. There is no money for that. Also, there is no transportation to build around that life style. The majority of those living in the Fringe have no car. So, there is only public transportation. And that is not a suitable way to engage a child in any sports practice or game.

The end result is that there is little to no relationship building with friends at school or on a sports team. Isolation and loneliness are a fringing child's world. She is already a bit of a mystery to fellow students. She is an outcast. And unfortunately, her fringing further perpetuates the mystery and seclusion.

Summers are particularly hard for a fringing child. In the summer for Ella, she often sits in her motel room with the curtains pulled while members of the family sleep. She is in the dark for most the day playing video games. She doesn't get to see her friend's daily like when school is in session. Since she doesn't live in their neighborhood, she isn't hanging out with others like the rest of the kids are.

Not only is she isolated and withdrawn (physically and emotionally), but her fringing is cultivating an even more strained teen-parent relationship. The bottom line is that a teen's perspective on her parental units is challenged enough during these trying teen years. Under the best of circumstances, this relationship is naturally riddled with angst, being misunderstood and seemingly oppressed by parents from growing up. Now add the emotional twists and turns of being homeless during those teen years.

Can you see resentment and anger building towards her parents? I sense the outcome for Ella and other homeless teens is a wicked sense of injustice and unfairness. Those feelings easily translate into anger. That anger can either motivate or destroy their future.

In short, her childhood is centered on trauma, seclusion, shame and embarrassment. Being raised in The Fringe will have a permanent impact on Ella's overall development. These traumatic living conditions are what I call "toxic stress." This toxic stress is real and has a measurable result on her life and all homeless children.

Here is the blatant reality of my emotionally charged feelings about the devastating impact that *my* life has on *my* child. There is no denying the harm I am causing. Don't think that I am obtuse to this fact! Guilt overwhelms me. Let me say that again. Guilt overwhelms me. As if a life of despair and shame aren't enough. Once you begin to live this life, there is no denying the seepage of turmoil, stress and devastation into the very being that is your child.

Although being raised in a home of abuse is no way to raise a child, being raised in The Fringe is no way to raise a child either. I have spent many nights contemplating the thought of giving up my child for adoption.

But I do have one reason that I haven't done so thus far, hope. I cling to the hope that I will not be homeless forever. Hope is not some trite expression that just rolls off my tongue. Hope is my sustenance.

This lifestyle directly impacts my child's development. This lifestyle directly impacts Ella's development. Better take note, friends. This directly impacts every classroom, in every school, in every city, in every state in our country. These children are our future. "Children experiencing homelessness are four times more likely to show delayed development. They also have twice the rate of learning disabilities as non-homeless children."[26]

Homelessness has a measurable effect on their emotional health as well. "Children experiencing homelessness have three times the rate of emotional and behavioral problems compared to non-homeless children. And among school-age homeless children 47% have problems such as anxiety, depression, and withdrawal, compared to 18% of other school-age children."[27]

And last but not least, it has an adverse impact on their physical health. "Children experiencing homelessness are sick four times more often than other children. They have four times as many respiratory infections, twice as many ear infections. And they have five times more gastrointestinal problems."[28]

In short, being raised in The Fringe, like Ella wrote, "robs her of her childhood." Where is the stability and the rhythm of consistency? Where is the joy? Where is the laughter? Where is the friendship? Where is the security? In what does she place her hope? How does she even cultivate hope?

The answer to many of the above questions is based on the child's perspective. That is the point after all of sharing Ella's story. Her answer to those questions is pivotal in understanding what it is

26 http://www.familyhomelessness.org/media/306.pdf, (page 5, November 25, 2014)
27 Ibid
28 http://www.familyhomelessness.org/media/306.pdf, (page 4, November 25, 2014)

like for a homeless child. Here comes the bone of contention: Ella will adamantly tell you she is NOT homeless. In facts of her reality, she is resentful of the "real" homeless and can't stand them. She thinks they are a disgrace in society, a littering of the streets with degradation and laziness. She can't imagine what their problem is, other than they choose to be homeless. (Sound familiar?)

For Ella, the fact remains that she believes she has a home. This is based on evidence of a residence in a motel with their own front door with running water and electricity. It's irrelevant how temporary her address is. It's irrelevant how many times they move in a year. This is her definition of a home, therefore, not homeless.

Unfortunately (or fortunately) steps have been taken with the McKinney Vento Act to ensure a uniform national description of what a homeless child is. Under that Act, a homeless child is defined as:

> "(2) The term homeless children and youths' —
> (A) means individuals who lack a fixed, regular, and adequate nighttime residence (within the meaning of section 103(a)(1)); and
> (B) includes —
> (i) children and youths who are sharing the housing of other persons due to loss of housing, economic hardship, or a similar reason; are living in motels, hotels, trailer parks, or camping grounds due to the lack of alternative adequate accommodations; are living in emergency or transitional shelters; are abandoned in hospitals; or are awaiting foster care placement;
> (ii) children and youths who have a primary nighttime residence that is a public or private place not designed for or ordinarily used as a regular sleeping accommodation for human beings (within the meaning of section 103(a)(2)(C));

(iii) children and youths who are living in cars, parks, public spaces, abandoned buildings, substandard housing, bus or train stations, or similar settings; and

(iv) migratory children (as such term is defined in section 1309 of the Elementary and Secondary Education Act of 1965) who qualify as homeless for the purposes of this subtitle because the children are living in circumstances described in clauses (i) through (iii)."[29]

Of the children living in motels, doubled up, and in transitional housing, 90% of them do not believe they are homeless. As well, most of the parents do not consider themselves to be homeless either. So what do we do? Do we go in there and convince them they are homeless and that they need to do something about it?

As I imagine, you probably agree that this isn't a realistic approach. Perhaps we have come so far so fast that this childlike perspective is what the new national definition of homeless should be based on.

That being said, the new national definition of a homeless person or child, would **not** be those living in motels, doubled up or in transitional housing. Is that realistic? Is there a new level of socioeconomic status that has emerged founded on the recession and housing market crash of the first ten years of the 2000's? Will our American society have a permanent people that are living in constant fear or state of flummox? Ella asserts that indeed a new people have emerged. It's like in the 80's when the term 'yuppie' was added to our language. A yuppie was a new socioeconomic class of young upwardly mobile professionals.

Perhaps it is time for the Urban Dictionary to add a new term for our times, **P**ermanently **A**daptive **T**emporarily **H**oused families. I proclaim **PATH** people, a brave people blazing a new trail, a new path in society. Ella is a first generation **PATH**. She may be living with toxic stress in a state of flummox, but she asserts she is

---

29   http://www2.ed.gov/policy/elsec/leg/esea02/pg116.html (pages 16-17)

not homeless and has as much a fighting chance to succeed in this world as any other child.

Oh how I digress, yet again. Is it easy to agree that she is not homeless? Perhaps the creation of our secret society was just the first step in the evolution of PATH people. Maybe society will make way for a new socioeconomic status? It is said by John Locke that, "As people are walking all the time, in the same spot, a path appears."

But until then, I must ask, now that we have a "poster child" for our cause will you take notice of our plight?

Do you feel inspired to help or are you relieved you may be able to accept Ella's view point and write off a large group of fringers to PATH? That is just the way their lives are and they just have to deal with it. What if PATH people are established as it's own class? What is society's response to them? What is the government's response and responsibility to them? By designating a PATH people, are we then able to adequately and fairly assess the situation of how to help them? They are a whole new level of those living not only in poverty, but living in extreme tenancy. That is poverty today in America.

By defining two sets of those in The Fringe, this allows us to re-class what or who is a "homeless" person. By doing so, then we can re-access, evaluate, define and engage in how to develop public policy to alleviate homelessness in our country.

The blessing of Ella's story is that this goes much deeper than contemplating giving money to a panhandler which is now on almost every street corner in our country. Ella's story beckons us to evaluate redefining who and why the poor are in our country. Only then can we come together as a morally conscience society to delve into the matters at hand.

After Ella risked being judged to share her story, will you judge a non-homeless (self proclaimed, and not by government definitions) PATH child the way you judge a homeless person begging on the corner? Do you tend to agree with Ella that there are levels and labels in The Fringe? Is there a natural grace given to this child raised in despair and poverty, and not to the beggar? Is it still so easy to write them off? Is that beggar on the corner so common place that we have de-evolved as a culture for which a beggar is a reminder of nothing, as John Berger says?

I think before society can accept a new social class and generation of PATH people, one has to cross the bridge to their side to walk a mile in their shoes. That is the point of breaking our silence. Can you help a homeless child or a PATH child cultivate hope? How can you possibly help? Keep asking questions. I don't have all the answers.

We need more people to tell their story, to walk alongside them a mile in their shoes. Maybe, mentor a homeless or PATH child? It makes all the difference. It's that simple. It's like Magic Johnson says, "All kids need is a little help, a little hope and someone who believes in them." That is how you cultivate hope, by believing in them.

You don't have to mentor the parents. You don't have to be afraid. You don't have to save them from blazing a new PATH or being homeless. You don't have to pay their hotel bill. You don't have to buy them clothes. You don't even have to agree on who is "really" homeless and who is a PATH person. Just cultivate a bit of hope in a child. Hope is the only thing that can truly break the cycle of poverty.

Even if you believe there are levels in The Fringe and some are acceptable and some are not, do you realize that the beggar is also someone's child? Don't forget to wonder what that beggar's story is. Is he Bud, fringe by death, the numb former police chief? Is he the unnamed "avid reader?" Is she Sabrina the gifted care giver? Or is it Ella's parents at the end of the month? We are all someone's children and we all deserve dignity and hope.

Don't judge Ella or her family. Dig deep to find out what life is like for others. That is what sharing our stories is about. May it not be for naught? Yes, I am asking you to go beyond reading our stories in this book. Go. Do. See. Learn. Those who risk to go will reap a great reward!

> *We cannot hold a torch to light another's path*
> *without brightening our own.*
> – Ben Sweetland[30]

30   http://www.brainyquote.com/quotes/keywords/path_3.html (December 1, 2014)

15 My Life Now

I contemplate which story of the members of The Fringe to tell next. Heavy on my mind is the grandmother living in the woods with her six grandchildren. They are the children of her daughter, the crack addict. I encountered Grandma and the children, ages 14 months to 12 years old, when a new shelter facility opened up in the area where we were fringing. There was no shelter within a 100 mile radius for women with children. When this shelter opened, the phrase, "they came out of the woodwork" literally applied.

But I am also considering sharing about this lovely family that I met that moved from Detroit to the west. There was the husband, wife, one son, and one daughter, who loves apple sauce! They had been hopping from state to state looking for jobs. They were determined to find a place with employment opportunities to make their new home. Reality for them is that the husband is a "blue-collar" machinist factory worker with skills that have quickly become irrelevant.

But instead of another story, perhaps it's time to just wrap this up. Yes, I think that may be so. I will have to save the stories of the others in The Fringe for another time. My energy level is dwindling and I am very tired. It's been quite the emotional roller coaster to relive these moments of my past.

I have to say that as I shuffle through the many encounters of the humble, scared and shamed people that are fringing, I am introspective now, just as you may be. Do you wonder what has happened to those whose stories I have already shared? I often wonder. It only takes that crescent moon hanging in the sky each month to bring me to wondering about the friends that came and went.

Unfortunately as the nature of our secret society goes regarding the stories of these people, I cannot provide an ending. I don't know where most of them are today. We are by necessity a very mobile, detached people. I don't know if most or any made it back into the building through that fast revolving door.

Many are probably still on the outside looking in. It is a hard and cruel part of our fringing life that our connections and encounters are so temporary and fleeting. As a matter of fact, it may be the toughest part. We lack community, belonging and relationships.

The only story I can offer at this point is back where we started, with my own. I am no longer a member of the secret society, The Fringe. I am one of the lucky ones that made it back through the fast revolving door. I allow myself to be labeled that glorious, overrated member of normal society now.

I have a job. I have a home, and even have a cat named Fringe. My son is growing up just as fast as your kids are. He doesn't remember much from our fringing days. There are times when I think that is a good thing. Then there are days when I realize I have written this bit of history as much for him as for my friends in The Fringe and my FOF (friends of The Fringe).

These stories and the history of their lives and challenges in The Fringe are for future generations like my son. I often wonder if my words to enlighten others on the hidden plight of those in The Fringe will be void. Maybe no one will read this book. Maybe no one really cares.

But, I know now that I was called to write about our lives. I was called to break down barriers and preconceived notions. I was called to break the silence. I was called to breathe life, dignity and respect into our troubled and complex existence.

Even as this book becomes old and gathers dust on shelves, I will cling to hope for those that are fringing. With every breath I take, I pray that they are living lives without judgment, persecution and shame in their struggle to survive life in the secret society.

Know that one day I will write more stories of those I met in The Fringe. That is once I beat this cancer and am living well again. I am just too tired to write more.

Perhaps my hope lies with my son, as well as those who have read this book, to continue my legacy to tell their stories if I don't make it.

Why is it that it takes nearly to the end of our time to reflect on the things in our lives that impacted us the most? I wonder why it took me so long to tell these stories. Why did it take till stage four cancer for me to realize that if I died without telling these stories my life would have been for naught.

Well, I can wonder these things but the fact is that my life in The Fringe prepared me for this time in my life.

I may have blocked out the pain and heartache of that part of my life and those I encountered while fringing for a long time. But the moment I heard the words "stage four cancer" they came flooding back. All of a sudden I knew it was time to tell my story and theirs.

You see the time I lost, or gained, depending on perspective, as a member of the secret society, The Fringe, prepared me. I know I can face this battle with cancer with the one thing that allowed me to escape life in The Fringe. **Hope.**

My life is a tribute to all things Fringe. My battle with cancer is all things Fringe. I am strong. I am a warrior. I am resilient. I am persistent. I am courageous. I am a survivor. I can hold my head up high and know that I can face the fight with dignity. I beat The Fringe. I beat the shame. I beat the persecution. I beat the judgment. I beat the isolation and loneliness.

I rose above. I conquered the norm and yet became the norm, and I will conquer cancer. I have hope. Hope is what I had while living in The Fringe. Hope is the one thing no one can take from you. Hope is the thing that binds people. Hope inspires. Hope admonishes norms. Hope tears down cultural walls. Hope allows us to care for those we don't understand. Hope allows us to ponder our being and the well being of others.

Dig deep, my son and my readers. Dig deep for the hope that all society will become kinder and less judgmental. Dig deep and live aware and not in ignorance. That is my hope for my son and for you.

Remember the crescent moon, our society's symbol? I ask that each time you see a crescent moon dangling in the night sky to think of those hanging on the edge of the whole of normal society…barely. Remember it as the secret society symbol for The Fringe.

Way back when I was in The Fringe, someone slipped into my hand a black onyx stone-carved crescent moon, and whispered the words, "Don't ever give up." I clutched that stone all the while fringing. Then I saved and stored that treasured crescent shaped stone for all these years.

When I was diagnosed with cancer, I took it out. Now I clutch to it again like a Catholic to a rosary.

I ask that you now remember the crescent moon for me a cancer warrior, still mysteriously hanging on to the whole of society and a normal life… barely. Seems some things never change. That crescent moon in the night sky symbolizes my courage. It also symbolizes that I always have hope.

My closing words (imagine me, that soprano opera singer, singing these words with my hands clasped tightly at my bosom), and you can quote me this time,

> *"Be a living example of compassion fueled by passion for excellence in kindness to all."*

> – mystery woman from The Fringe
> (and back)

Homeless Stars

(The key to Famous Former Fringe Members in the front of the book.)

Steve Jobs http://abcnews.go.com/Business/photos/jim-cramer-celebrities-homeless-16581069/image-16581164

Steve Harvey http://www.businessinsider.com/rich-and-famous-people-who-were-homeless- (December 7, 2014)

Jim Carrey http://www.businessinsider.com/rich-and-famous-people-who-were-homeless- (December 7, 2014)

Kelly Clarkson http://abcnews.go.com/Business/photos/jim-cramer-celebrities-homeless-16581069/image-16581164

Michael Oher (*Blind Side* movie) http://www.businessinsider.com/rich-and-famous-people-who-were-homeless- (December 7, 2014)

Halle Berry http://www.businessinsider.com/rich-and-famous-people-who-were-homeless- (December 7, 2014)

Jewel http://www.businessinsider.com/rich-and-famous-people-who-were-homeless- (December 7, 2014)

Chris Gardner (*The Pursuit of Happiness* movie) http://www.businessinsider.com/rich-and-famous-people-who-were-homeless- (December 7, 2014)

Ella Fitzgerald http://www.businessinsider.com/rich-and-famous-people-who-were-homeless- (December 7, 2014)

Cappadonna http://www.complex.com/music/2014/06/rappers-who-used-to-be-homeless/2pac

Kurt Cobain http://rollingout.com/entertainment/a-list-celebrities-who-were-once-homeless/attachment/kurt-cobain-2/

Harry Houdini http://www.businessinsider.com/rich-and-famous-people-who-were-homeless- (December 7, 2014)

Kelsey Grammer http://www.projectcasting.com/news/15-celebrities-who-were-once-homeless/

2Pac http://www.complex.com/music/2014/06/rappers-who-used-to-be-homeless/2pac

David Letterman http://rollingout.com/entertainment/a-list-ce-lebrities-who-were-once-homeless/attachment/david_letterman/
Lil'Kim http://www.complex.com/music/2014/06/rappers-who-used-to-be-homeless/2pac
William Shatner http://rollingout.com/entertainment/a-list-ce-lebrities-who-were-once-homeless/attachment/william-shatner-9480789-1-402/
Al Pacino http://rollingout.com/entertainment/a-list-celebri-ties-who-were-once-homeless/attachment/al-pacino-3/
Hillary Swank http://www.businessinsider.com/rich-and-famous-people-who-were-homeless- (December 7, 2014)
Shania Twain http://newsfeed.time.com/2013/07/11/stars-who-were-once-homeless/slide/shania-twain/
Jennifer Lopez http://www.businessinsider.com/rich-and-famous-people-who-were-homeless- (December 7, 2014)
Drew Carey http://www.businessinsider.com/rich-and-famous-people-who-were-homeless- (December 7, 2014)
Margot Kidder http://www.ranker.com/list/celebrities-who-fell-into-homelessness/polkadotking?for-mat=SLIDESHOW&page=9
Sugar Ray Williams http://www.ranker.com/list/celebrities-who-fell-into-homelessness/polkadotking?for-mat=SLIDESHOW&page=9
Willie Aames http://www.ranker.com/list/celebrities-who-fell-into-homelessness/polkadotking?for-mat=SLIDESHOW&page=9
Suze Orman http://www.businessinsider.com/rich-and-famous-people-who-were-homeless- (December 7, 2014)
Daniel Craig http://www.businessinsider.com/rich-and-famous-people-who-were-homeless- (December 7, 2014)
Phil McGraw (*Dr. Phil*) http://www.businessinsider.com/rich-and-famous-people-who-were-homeless- (December 7, 2014)

Different?

Off the beaten track?

Positively Weird?

But it's solid art?

Look for it!
Publish it!
at
Eucatastrophe Press
eucatastrophepress.com

MORE FICTION FROM ENERGION PUBLICATIONS IMPRINTS

Enzar Empire Press

Tales from Jevlir: Oddballs	Henry E. Neufeld	$9.99
Day of the Dragon	Joseph G. Whelan	$24.99

enzarempire.com

Eucatastrophe Press

Megabelt (2nd Edition)	Nick May	$12.99
Minutemen (2nd Edition)	Nick May	$12.99
Molecricket (Hardcover)	Nick May	$34.99
The Fringe	Renee Crosby	$9.99

eucatastrophepress.com

Energion Publications

Allegheny Hideaway	Kimberly Gordon	$16.99
Covenant	Daniel Martin	$17.99
Please Love Me	Kimberly Gordon	$14.99
Prayer Trilogy	Kimberly Gordon	$9.99
The Traveler's Advance	Heath Taws	$14.99
Stories of the Way	Henry E. Neufeld	$9.99

energion.com

Generous Quantity Discounts Available
Dealer Inquiries Welcome
Energion Publications — P.O. Box 841
Gonzalez, FL 32560
Website: energion.com
Phone: (850) 525-3916

www.ingramcontent.com/pod-product-compliance
Lightning Source LLC
Chambersburg PA
CBHW022041170626
46808CB00003B/1318